# URDU

## THE BEST STORIES OF OUR TIMES

OTHER BOOKS IN THE SERIES

Telugu

# URDU

## THE BEST STORIES OF OUR TIMES

EDITED AND TRANSLATED BY

RAKHSHANDA JALIL

HARPERPERENNIAL

*An Imprint of* HarperCollins *Publishers*

First published in India by Harper Perennial 2023
An imprint of HarperCollins *Publishers*
4th Floor, Tower A, Building No. 10, DLF Cyber City,
DLF Phase II, Gurugram, Haryana – 122002
www.harpercollins.co.in
2 4 6 8 10 9 7 5 3 1



P-ISBN: 978-93-5699-382-2
E-ISBN: 978-93-5699-383-9



Typeset in 11.5/16.2 Adobe Caslon Pro at
Manipal Technologies Limited, Manipal

Printed and bound at
Replika Press Pvt. Ltd.

MIX
Paper from responsible sources
FSC® C016779

This book is produced from independently certified FSC® paper to ensure responsible forest management.

# CONTENTS

# INTRODUCTION

I MUST BEGIN BY thanking Rahul Soni, my editor at HarperCollins, for broaching the idea of this collection in the first place. In the course of the months and years of its gestation (yes, indeed, this book has taken a long time to come to fruition), we were clear we didn't want a representative sampling of Urdu fiction that begins with the early stalwarts of the Urdu short story, namely Premchand, Ahmad Nadeem Qasmi and Ghulam Abbas, going on to the 'four pillars' of modern Urdu short fiction, that is, Saadat Hasan Manto, Ismat Chughtai, Rajinder Singh Bedi and Krishan Chander, and only then come to more contemporary writers. We wanted this volume to focus on modern writing, preferably from the 1990s onwards, as those years were marked by many social and political upheavals. We were curious how, and to what extent, these changes would find reflection in the works of the Urdu afsana-nigar.

Any selection is, by its very definition, subjective. No matter how much an editor professes an unblemished, clear-sighted objectivity, personal likes and dislikes do creep in and influence who is included and who isn't. So, while broadly speaking I have tried to stay true to the spirit of my initial conversations with Rahul: that this should be a selection of the finest modern writings from India and that we mustn't go by what has been most anthologized assuming that it is, necessarily, the finest – either among the genre of the Urdu short story itself or the oeuvre of a particular writer. No, instead the criteria for a collection such as this should be good prose, a range of concerns, divergent points of view that, taken together, reflect the currents that ripple through modern India. And just as Urdu is not the language of India's Muslims alone, these stories need not be about Muslims; instead, they should reflect a mood, an outlook, a catholicity of concerns among Urdu writers.

Urdu belongs to neither a single state nor a single community – it is a language of the people, by the people, for the people. It is ready to belong to whoever is willing to step forward and claim it. For far too long, the doomsayers have been predicting the end of Urdu and a whole way of life that accompanied it. The Urdu–Hindi debate has divided Urdu-wallahs and Hindi-wallahs into warring champions occupying opposite ends of a Great Divide, a bit like wrestlers in an akhada. Yet, despite the formidable odds stacked against it, Urdu has not merely survived but flourished. Yes, fewer people read it in its own script. Yes, its propagation is not tied to employment generation. Yes, the government has paid mere lip service to safeguarding its interests. Yes, many of those who nod their heads in appreciation when they hear Urdu poetry being read or recited or a dastan being rendered in the time-honoured and stylized way of the dastango of yesteryears possibly do so because it sounds dramatic and moving rather than because they fully understand the real meaning of those mellifluous words. But that is not to say that Urdu is dead or dying; it is not merely alive but has managed to remain relevant. It is still the language of the heart and soul of India as this collection of stories by writers from different parts of the country demonstrates.

Let us begin with the two senior-most writers in this collection: Surendra Prakash (1930–2002) and Qurratulain Hyder (1927–2007). One might think they wouldn't feature in a collection of 'modern' Urdu stories, but I chose to include them precisely because of the topical nature of the stories I have selected from their oeuvre. In '*Bajooka*' (meaning scarecrow), published in the collection entitled *Baazgoi* in 1988, Surendra Prakash tips his hat to Premchand's Hori, the protagonist of the famous novel *Godaan* published in 1936. By the time Surendra Prakash picks up the story a half century later: 'The Hori of Premchand's story had become so old that even the hair on his eyebrows and eyelashes had turned white. His back was bent, and the veins stood out on his dark, calloused hands.' While much has changed in modern

India, the lives of farmers and the rural poor continue to be marked by deprivation and despair. New motifs are added to old themes of exploitation and socio-economic disparities:

> Two sons had been born to him over the years; neither was alive now. One had drowned in the Ganga while bathing; the other had been killed in a police encounter. Why he was 'encountered' by the police is not really a matter worth recounting. Whenever a person comes to acknowledge his own self and begins to sense the disquiet that is all around him, an encounter with the police is only natural. Something of this sort happened to Hori's son too … Old Hori's hands, holding the plough, loosened momentarily and trembled a little, but then their grasp tightened. He called out to his oxen, and the teeth of his plough tore through the earth and moved along the furrow.

As the country grapples with agrarian unrest and the draconian farm laws (since repealed) nibble away the rights of the farmers, Surendra Prakash's '*Bajooka*' presents a dystopian nightmare of what else awaits the beleaguered Indian farmer.

Qurratulain Hyder's 'The Halfway View' ('*Nazara Darmiyan Hai*') is located in cosmopolitan Bombay (or 'Bambayi' as it is pronounced in Urdu) where Harry Belafonte's 'Jamaica Farewell' plays amidst the chatter of 'West-obsessed' Indian women in a Cumballa Hill skyscraper; clearly, it was written well before the cut-off date of the 1990s that I had set for myself, but such is the timeless quality of this story that I felt compelled to include it here. It features a love triangle between Piroja, a down-at-heel Parsi girl from Tardeo who is also a gifted pianist, an impoverished Khurshid Alam who makes a marriage of convenience with Almas, the spoilt daughter of a fabulously wealthy Bombay businessman. Flitting in and out of this story, like a little firefly, is young Tarabai, blind from birth, but gifted with new sight by a twist of fate and the miracle of medicine and science.

'The Circumcision of Khalid' ('*Khalid ka Khatna*') by Ghazanfar (b. 1953) takes us to small-town India: relatives have gathered from far and near, a middle-class home is beautifully decorated, a young Muslim boy's rite of passage is about to take place in the khatna ceremony that marks the circumcision and is traditionally conducted amidst much rejoicing, with feasting for the extended family and neighbours. However, this happy occasion is marred by the boy's terror because one day his father had told him that 'goons kill those who have had a circumcision'. The boy's statement falls like a bolt of lightning on the assembled guests: 'Ghastly scenes of search-and-find operations rose before their eyes. Bodies stripped naked. Knives thrust into chests.' Ghazanfar's story carries echoes of the Partition-related violence in Manto's haiku-like story 'Mishtake' in *Black Margins.* It would appear that the more things change the more they remain the same over a span of seventy-five years or so and, as far as communal violence is considered, we as a nation have made no 'progress'!

Zakia Mashhadi (b. 1944) takes us by the hand and leads us into the heart of rural India, to a land so impoverished that members of the Musahar community catch and eat rats for want of other means of sustenance. Musahar belong to a Dalit community found in the eastern Gangetic Plain and the Terai.

Their name literally means 'rat-eater' due to their main occupation being catching rats and eating them, such being their destitution. Due to their occupation and the fact that they eat the rats they catch, they occupy the lowest rung in the socio-economic and caste pyramid. They are easy prey for party functionaries who are tasked with finding enough poor men to form processions when a show of strength is required in big cities. Carrying flags and chanting '*Inquilab Zindabad*' ('Long Live the Revolution'), they are pulled out of villages, given rubber chappals, a few measly rupees and the promise of a full meal:

> There were many of them. Like rats driven out of their holes. They made up nearly a half-mile-long procession. Each one was carrying a flag in his hand. By now, the sherbet had reached their bellies. For a long time they had been shouting 'jindabad-jindabad'. After every twenty to twenty-five men, there would be a worker like Mishrji who would raise the cry of 'inquilab'. Who knew what 'inquilab' meant? Puri-sabzi, sherbet, or simply a fat rat!

In the hands of a lesser writer, this would simply have been a soliloquy on the sharp poverty that lurks in rural pockets in India's vast hinterland. In the hands of a writer as gifted as Zakia Mashhadi, 'A Rat's Death' (the original title being '*Eik Makaude ki Maut*') becomes a requiem for a lost life and the sheer callousness and greed of an uncaring 'system'.

With 'The Stone Age' ('*Stone Age*' in Urdu) by Gulzar (b. 1934), we travel to Afghanistan and a world of falling mortar shells, crumbling cities, maimed children, mutilated corpses, fleeing people rendered refugees in their own home in the face of relentless attacks by the fidayeen. While the rest of the world marches on, one set of people – forced by circumstances beyond their control and powers they cannot comprehend – are pushed backwards in time, into regression:

> In the beginning of time, men made weapons out of stone. They hunted for food and lived in caves. Those clans that had fire would be considered superior to others. They moved to open grounds, travelled and conquered new territories…
>
> Naseer was preparing a stone weapon by rubbing a small, sharp stone against a bigger stone.

In a scenario reminiscent of Samuel Beckett's nihilist play *Waiting for Godot*, 'The Halted Train' ('*Deir Se Achanak Ruki Huwi Gaadi*') by Abdus Samad (b. 1952) dwells on the idea of the meaninglessness of all existence and all effort that might bring an end to waiting. Somewhere in the vast country that is India, a passenger train has halted suddenly and inexplicably in the middle of nowhere causing much consternation among the travellers, especially since these are troubled times and there's an ominous sense of dread about what lies outside the shuttered compartment. The garrulous passengers cannot stop talking amongst themselves about: the possible reasons why the train has stopped, the dangers that lurk outside, the need for someone to go out and explore, the need to take remedial action in future, to lodge complaints with competent authorities, and so on and so forth. But all the bombast and rhetoric of the long cyclical conversations ends – not with a bang – but a whimper:

'It means nothing … Really, it is very simple: we will keep on talking till this train moves again.'

'Even if someone were to die of hunger, thirst, or some other reason?'

'You don't need a reason to die; you just need an excuse.'

Syed Muhammad Ashraf (b. 1957) is known to draw on India's rich cultural past to weave stories that seamlessly bring the past and the present together. 'The Last Exile' ('*Aakhri Banbaas*') is one such story, at once timeless and yet rooted in the here and now. The eldest in a family inherits an ancient manuscript that foretells that a very special being will be granted the blessed darshan when the end is nigh. He travels to be with that being in his last moments so that he too can catch a glimpse of that divine sight and partake of the Infinite Joy of Paradise in this very life. Ashraf's story will confound those who think the Urdu writer dwells entirely in an Urdu-speaking milieu or speaks only of the concerns of Muslims, for there is no trace of an Urdu-speaking culture, or of Muslims, for that matter, in the entire story.

The brutality and inhumanity of the modern metropolis is the theme of 'A Night's Paradise' ('*Eik Raat ki Jannat*') by Faiyaz Riffat (1940–2022). A nameless young man comes to the big city with dreams in his eyes, but he is snatched by death when he is at the pinnacle of youth:

> Weakened by hunger and starvation, he had been swept away like a twig in a gust of wind. And with him were gone his dreams and aspirations, lost forever in some surging unknown ocean.

> He had come to the city with such dreams, but now those dreams lay trampled in the dust. The dazzling city lights, the buildings that reached up to the sky, the array of beautiful faces – all remained strangers to him.

But what follows this untimely death is entirely unexpected. Or perhaps not so in a big, brutal city.

Khalid Jawed's (b. 1960) long-nurtured and well-documented fascination with death and disease reaches an apogee in 'A Letter of Condolence for the Living' ('*Zindon ke Liye Eik Taziyatnama*'). A sick, ailing man, with a stone in his kidney, has an intense, burning need to urinate but he cannot because he finds himself in a new-age city that is so immaculately clean, so fragrant with the smell of flowers and detergents that he finds no place where he can relieve himself. What is more, in this surreal post-modernist fable, this new world order has rid itself of all manner of filth, including bodily functions. There are no urinals, public or private, because men have done away with the need to flush out all the waste and toxins that they used to once carry around on their person. Having gained control over the body's frailties and its related abominations and impurities, men have caused death to scurry away with its tail between its legs:

> … death is a thing of the past. Only he who has become filthy or will spread filth will die. Death must be lying somewhere on the rubbish heap of history; now, there aren't even any rats left in the world to nibble away at it.

We return to the big city in Salam Bin Razzaq's 'Life is Not a Story' ('*Zindagi Afsana Nahin*') but this time to a distinctly Muslim milieu, a milieu that few Muslim writers wish to acknowledge let alone write about with such clarity and empathy. Salam Bin Razzaq (b. 1941) talks of prickly subjects such as the lack of family planning among Muslims and the large number of children, its consequences on the health of women, the inability to provide for many children, the high dropout rate among children from the lower socio-economic strata, the link between unemployment and excessive religiosity, non-consensual marital sex, the foisting of the burqa on young women by patriarchal males, among other such subjects that are usually brushed under the carpet. Because life is not a story, what might well have been a sweet love story between two young lovers, Jamila and Aslam, is destined to unspool as a tragedy of our times. As Salam Bin Razzaq notes ruefully:

> But, dear readers, Life is not a story! A fiction writer has the right to end his story wherever he wishes or turn it in any direction he chooses. But no one has control over the swift and strong currents of Life – not even the writer! Sometimes, the current of Life is so strong that the writer's pen is swept away like a twig. Something like that happened here too.

Anwar Qamar (b. 1941) picks up the thread of communalism that runs like a canker through the fabric of Indian society in 'What Happened on the Ship' ('*Jahaaz Par Kya Huwa*'). No names are taken, no dates are given, but we can safely surmise that the story is located in the immediate aftermath of the horrific communal carnage in Gujarat that has caused a group of desperate men, women and children to flee their homes as stowaways in a cargo ship making its way from the Kandla port on the western coast to distant Kolkata in hope of finding a safe haven under the Marxist government in the state of West Bengal. The setting is a battered old ship named, appropriately enough, the MV *Gandhi*; it is on its last legs before being sent for dry docking. Mention of the film *Schindler's List*, memories of the communal violence of 1947 by an elderly Punjabi Partition survivor, and references to the Urdu writer Krishan Chander's collection of short stories entitled *Hum Wahshi Hain* (*We Are Barbarians*) combine to tell us there has always been a barbarian lurking in the human heart, and good and evil have always coexisted: sometimes one has the upper hand, sometimes another. For every act of inhumanity perpetrated by one set of humans on another, there will always be some human being who will be willing to rise above and beyond the call of duty to serve humanity.

Khurshid Akram's (b. 1963) 'Suffocation' ('*Habs*') is located in an overcrowded bus which becomes a microcosm of the human condition: there is beauty and plenty, vastness and openness outside; inside the bus there is want and deprivation. There is also the pettiness and lack of civility that comes with overcrowding, for it is very difficult to be mindful of others when one is standing on one leg, barely able to breathe inside a shuttered and suffocating enclosed space. The story can be read at multiple levels, one of them being for old and new migrants, how new migrants who have succeeded in getting into a prized new land (legally or illegally) are so resentful of others who have come after them. In the following lines, the bus could be replaced with any such prized space:

> But those who had already boarded the bus tried to stop the newcomers from entering.
>
> 'Brother, why are you getting in? You can see there is no space,' said one man who had only very recently managed to get in himself. The ones below were insistent upon getting in, come what may. Their bodies were bathed in sweat. The women were the worst affected in that crush. Sometimes, they would turn around and glare at the men who were taking advantage of the terrible crowd and leaning against them.

Tariq Chhatari (b. 1954) writes with empathy and a close understanding of the qasbas and small towns of north India. He has experienced at first hand the 'mili-juli tehzeeb', the multicultural pluralistic way of life that was once the norm rather than the exception. He writes with anguish when he sees that secular fabric getting frayed and ripped by divisive forces. His story, 'The Line' ('*Lakeer*'), is both a paean to a lost culture and tradition, and a cry of anguish at its loss. As with Syed Muhammad Ashraf's 'The Last Exile', the minute and detailed descriptions of Hindu customs and beliefs, the attention to details, the use of correct terms and descriptions demonstrates the catholicity of the Urdu writers and the extent to which they have absorbed the 'other' within their own psyche. Sample this:

> Hameed was the son of Faqir Muhammad. He had run away from his school at the mosque to sit in his neighbour Pandit Brij Kishore's pathshala. Pandit Brij Kishore loved him dearly, more than all his other pupils, and affectionately called him

Kanhaiya. Hameed dreamt of Krishna and the Ashtami festival, and rocked his thoughts like the idol of infant Krishna being rocked in its gilded crib.

Communalism, and the violence it spawns in civil society, is a recurring concern for the Urdu writer. Ali Imam Naqvi (1945–2014) locates his story in what we presume is Mumbai scarred by communal violence though again, as in Anwar Qamar's 'What Happened on the Ship', no details are mentioned; perhaps none are necessary in this bone-chilling story told from the perspective of Parsi corpse bearers. 'The Vultures of Doongerwadi' ('*Doongerwadi ke Giddh*') tells you simply and baldly that the vultures will go wherever there are corpses: be it in the Parsi tower of silence or the streets of a city. Nothing more needs to be said, for the vultures, after all, are nature's best scavengers; they do their job well. It matters little to them if there are Parsi corpses to be pecked upon or Hindu and Muslim ones to feast on.

As editor of this volume, I make no claim that this collection represents the 'best' Urdu short fiction. For, after all, what is 'best'? Who decides? And how? Using which parameters? As a translator and as a close and faithful reader I can, however, say with utmost sincerity that this is a fair sampling of some of the finest voices in modern Urdu fiction. I hope I have managed, to some extent, convey the range of concerns and topics, not to mention styles and genres. More importantly, I hope that a collection such as this goes some way in busting the myth of homogeneity, that Urdu writing is concerned with Muslims alone or with other-worldly subjects such as ishq/mohabbat or Sufism and spirituality. It is annoying when well-meaning people mouth platitudes to defend Urdu or proclaim their love for the language: '*Urdu zubaan ishq aur mohabbat ki zubaan hai*' ('Urdu is the language of love and romance'). That, to my mind, is not just banal but also limiting; for not just Urdu poetry but all of Urdu literature is concerned with not one or two but a variety of concerns. But because stereotypes have greater reach and penetration than ground reality, not many are able to shake Urdu loose from the escapist fantasy of popular perception; the few who manage to do so see Urdu for what it is: a real, living, tensile language forever willing to adapt, to replenish and renew itself.

**Rakhshanda Jalil**
September 2023
New Delhi

# SCARECROW

*Surendra Prakash*

THE HORI OF Premchand's story had become so old that even the hair on his eyebrows and eyelashes had turned white. His back was bent, and the veins stood out on his dark, calloused hands.

Two sons had been born to him over the years; neither was alive now. One had drowned in the Ganga while bathing; the other had been killed in a police encounter. Why he was 'encountered' by the police is not really a matter worth recounting. Whenever a person comes to acknowledge his own self and begins to sense the disquiet that is all around him, an encounter with the police is only natural. Something of this sort happened to Hori's son too … Old Hori's hands, holding the plough, loosened momentarily and trembled a little, but then their grasp tightened. He called out to his oxen, and the teeth of his plough tore through the earth and moved along the furrow.

The sons had a wife each, and five children in all: the one who had died from drowning in the Ganga had three, and the other, who had been killed in the police encounter, had two. The burden of looking after all of them had fallen entirely on Hori, and the blood in his veins had begun to course through his old body with greater vigour.

That day, the sky was redder than usual even though the sun had not risen yet. The five children sat, stark naked, bathing around the well in Hori's courtyard. Hori's elder daughter-in-law was drawing water from the well and pouring it over them. The children were jumping, rubbing their belly and splashing water. The younger daughter-in-law was cooking large rotis and stacking them in a basket. And Hori was inside, changing his clothes and tying his turban. He finished tying his turban and looked at his face in the mirror placed in a small niche in the wall … his face was covered with wrinkles. Then he looked at the small photograph of Hanumanji hanging nearby, folded his hands, closed his eyes, and bowed his head. Thereafter, he came out into the courtyard and asked, 'Are you ready?'

'Yes, Bapu!' All the children chimed in unison. Both the daughters-in-law adjusted the veil over their head and began to work industriously. Hori saw that no one was ready yet. Everyone was lying. And he thought how important lies were to live one's life. Had God not granted lies to us as a boon, people would be falling dead like flies. They would have no reason to live. First, we lie, and then we stay alive in order to try and turn the lie into truth.

Take the case of Hori's grandchildren and his two daughters-in-law ... how busy they were in turning the lie they had just uttered into truth. By the time Hori picked up the sickles lying in one corner of the courtyard, they were all actually ready.

The fields were lush and ripe. The crop was ready. It was time to cut the harvest. It seemed like a festival, such was their excitement to reach the fields. As they were leaving, they noticed that the golden rays of the sun had bathed the entire house in a magical glow.

Hori adjusted the cloth on his shoulder and mused, 'What a good time this is! There is no threat from the government functionary, nor fear of the moneylender. No tyranny of the British rulers, nor a share owing to the landlord!' Green sheaves of wheat danced before his eyes.

'Come, Babu!' His elder grandson clutched his finger, and the other children crowded around his legs. The elder daughter-in-law closed the door to the room and the younger one placed the bundle of rotis on her head.

Invoking the name of Hanuman to bring them good luck, they came out of the main door and into the alley. Then turning right, they set off towards their field.

Some hustle and bustle had begun in the village lanes and alleys. People were going to and from the fields. One could tell that their hearts were bursting with happiness. Their eyes gleamed as they gazed upon their fields. Hori felt as though life was different today than what it was in the past. He turned back to look at the children following him. The lads looked exactly like children of farmers do: sallow complexioned, somewhat emaciated ... the sort of children who get scared at the sound of approaching jeeps or the coming of seasons. Both daughters-in-law looked exactly like widowed wives of poor farmers do: their face hidden by long veils, poverty lurking like lice in every crease of their crumpled clothes.

With his head bowed, Hori began to move forward. The fields lay spread out beyond the last house in the village. The Persian wheel stood silent nearby. A dog lay fast asleep under a neem tree. Some cows, buffaloes and oxen were snorting and eating from their troughs in a barn close by. Fields of golden wheat lay ahead. Beyond them, and after crossing a small stream, was Hori's field, where the crop stood ready.

Walking on the narrow footpaths, they looked like small bundles of different coloured clothes crawling on dry grass ... they were all heading to their field. Beyond that lay a stretch of barren land, which had some lifeless quicksand but not the slightest trace of greenery. Your feet would sink in it if you set foot on it. And the soil had become dry and crumbly just like the ashes from the pyre of Hori's two sons, when their bodies had burnt to fine ash that would scatter at the merest touch of a hand. The barren piece of land was gradually increasing. Hori could remember how it had expanded by two hands' width over the past fifty years. He hoped that the barren patch should not reach his field until his grandchildren came of age; by then he – Hori – too would be dead and gone, part of some wasteland himself!

The endless network of footpaths, and Hori and his family walking barefoot on them...

The sun was peering from the western window in the sky.

They had been walking for so long now that their feet were coated with dust. People on either side of the footpath were busy harvesting their crop. They would call out a greeting to the passersby and then resume slicing the stalks with their sickles, keeping the harvested stems to one side with a strange zeal and passion.

They crossed the stream one by one. There was barely any water in the stream. The sandy mud at the bottom was caked and dry; distinctive patterns were visible on its surface. These were the imprints of the water's feet. Up ahead, the lush green field could be seen. The sight lifted everyone's spirits. When the crop is harvested their courtyard will be filled with straw, the storeroom filled with grain, and how wonderful it will be to sit on the cot and eat rice to one's heart's content! How they will burp with delight once their bellies are full: the thought occurred to all of them almost simultaneously.

Suddenly, Hori stopped in his tracks. The rest of them also stopped. Hori was looking at his field in amazement. The others too were looking at Hori's face and then turning around to look at the field, when suddenly Hori moved forward with lightning speed. In a loud voice he called out, 'Hey, you … Who is there?'

They turned to look, but there was no answer. By now they had reached quite close to their field; they could clearly hear the sound of a sickle slashing through the crop at the far end of the field.

'Who is there? You bastard! Why don't you speak?' And Hori held aloft the sickle in his hand.

Suddenly a skeletal frame emerged from the other end of the field and looked at them with a smile. Then its voice was heard:

'It's me, Hori Kaka … The scarecrow,' it answered as it waved the sickle in its hand in the air.

A muffled cry of terror escaped the little group of people. Their faces turned waxen, and Hori turned white till his lips. For a few moments, they were all immobilized by terror. They stood silently.

No one can say for how long – a moment, a century, an age? None of them could say. Till they heard Hori's voice – quivering with anger – they were oblivious of their own existence.

'You … scarecrow … you! I created you to guard the field. I built you out of bamboo stalks. I put those clothes on you, clothes belonging to that English hunter on whose hunts my father used to go to call out the animals. And when the English hunter was leaving, he gave his torn, old khaki clothes to my father as a parting gift. I made your face from an old, disused pot from my house. I placed the English hunter's old hat on that face. You lifeless creature! *You* are cutting my crop!'

Hori spoke as he was moving towards the scarecrow, which was, as always, smiling at him as though Hori's words had not had the slightest effect upon him. As Hori came closer, he saw that nearly one-fourth of the crop had been harvested, and the scarecrow stood beside it, holding the sickle in its hand, smiling. They were surprised. How did it get hold of a sickle? They had been seeing it for months. It had always stood there empty-handed. But today … today it appeared human. A human being of flesh and blood like themselves! Hori nearly became mad with rage at this sight. He stepped forward and gave a mighty push to the scarecrow. But the scarecrow didn't budge an inch from its place. If anything, Hori himself fell back from the impact of his own force. His family ran, shouting, towards him. Holding his waist with his hands, he tried to get to his feet. Everyone rushed to help Hori. Terrified, he looked at the scarecrow and said, 'You! … You scarecrow! You have even become stronger than me? Me? … I, who made you with my own hands! I, who made you to protect my crops!'

As always, the scarecrow was smiling. He said, 'You are getting angry for no reason, Hori Kaka. I have merely cut my share of the harvest. One-fourth…'

'What right do you have in my children's share? Who are you?'

'It is my right, too, Hori Kaka … Because I am … because I protected this field.'

'But I had planted you here thinking you were lifeless. And lifeless things have no rights. And where did you get this sickle that you are holding in your hand?'

The scarecrow let out a hearty laugh. 'You are truly very simple, Hori Kaka! Here you are talking to me, and you think I am lifeless?'

'But who gave you this sickle and this life? I certainly didn't give either to you.'

'I got it on my own … the day you split the bamboo stalks to make me! When you got me the torn, old clothes belonging to the English hunter! The day you painted eyes and ears on that old, disused pot from your home! That very day, Life was quivering in all these things. They came together to create me. I stood here as the crops ripened. Slowly, gradually, a sickle emerged from my entire being. By the time the crop had ripened, the sickle was in my hand. But I have not been dishonest with what you left in my safekeeping. I was waiting for this day. Today, you have come to harvest your crop, I have cut my share. What is there to get angry in this?' The scarecrow spoke slowly so that everyone present could understand what he was saying.

'No, this can't be. This is trickery; I don't consider you a living being. I will ask the panchayat to take a decision on this. Throw your sickle. I won't let you take even a grain of my harvest…' Hori shouted. And the scarecrow threw the sickle, smiling.

The panchayat assembled at the village chaupal. The village headman and five elders were present. Hori was there along with his daughters-in-law and grandchildren. His face was crumpled with grief. His daughters-in-law stood to one side with the other women from the village. Everyone was waiting for the scarecrow. The panchayat was supposed to announce its decision today. The two parties to the dispute had both presented their sides of the case.

Finally, from a distance the scarecrow was spotted coming slowly, leisurely. Everyone turned to look at it. As always, it was smiling. The moment it entered the chaupal, everyone stood up unthinkingly and bowed their heads respectfully. Hori saw this and trembled with rage. He felt as though the scarecrow had bought the conscience of the entire village and the justice of the panchayat. He felt like a man struggling to stay afloat in fast-flowing water.

Finally, the senior-most member of the panchayat announced his decision. Hori's entire being trembled. He had to agree to give one-fourth of his harvest to the scarecrow. Then he stood to his feet and addressed his grandsons:

'Listen ... This is probably the last harvest of our lives. The barren land is still some distance from our field. I am telling you: don't ever make a scarecrow to safeguard your crops. Next year, when the oxen plough the field, the seeds are planted, and the nectar of rain causes tiny buds to sprout, tie me to a bamboo pole and plant me in the field ... in place of the scarecrow. I will protect your field until the wasteland stretches and devours your fertile soil and makes it dry and barren. Don't remove me from there ... Let me be there so that when people look at me, they are reminded not to make scarecrows. For the scarecrow is not lifeless ... It gets life on its own and its very being hands him a sickle, and he gets one-fourth of the harvest.'

And with these words, Hori walked slowly towards his field. His grandchildren were behind him, followed by his daughters-in-law and the rest of the people from the village. Everyone was walking with bowed head.

Hori fell down and died as he reached his field. His grandchildren began to tie him to a bamboo. The rest of the people stood watching the spectacle. The scarecrow took off the hunter's hat from his head and held it to its breast. It bowed its head.

# THE HALFWAY VIEW

*Qurratulain Hyder*

TARABAI'S EYES ARE as bright as the stars as she looks at everything around her with wonderment. Actually, Tarabai's face is all eyes. She's a thin, starving girl, a victim of famine, who has been working at Begum Almaas Khurshid Alam's home for only a few months. She looks at the luxurious things stocked in her mistress's flat with eyes wide open for she has never seen such luxury and opulence – not even in her wildest dreams. She is a child widow from a village near Gorakhpur. She has been called here to Bombay, after the death of her parents and in-laws, by her uncle who works as a milkman in the city.

Almaas Begum has been married for barely three or four months. When the Mangalorean ayah who had come with her from her parents' home went back to her 'native' place, Almaas Begum's highly efficient aunt, Begum Usmani, who was also a well-known social worker, called up the Employment Exchange and Tarabai arrived, blinking her eyes like a firefly, at the tenth floor of Gul Nastran, the Cumballa Hill skyscraper. Almaas Begum found Tarabai to be satisfactory in every way. However, when the other servants addressed her as 'Tarabai', she took great offense. 'Am I a singing-dancing girl?' Tarabai protested. But now she has got accustomed to being called Tara*bai* instead of Tara*dai*, and remains quietly engrossed in her work when she is not gazing, wide-eyed, at her Begum and her Sahab.

If Almaas Begum had her way, she wouldn't let her stylish husband out of her sight. Nor was she in favour of keeping a nubile young maid in her house. But she made no protest at the choice of her experienced aunt when she saw the emaciated but skilful and hard-working Tarabai.

In the mornings, Tarabai would bring tea to the bedroom, and with great devotion, polish Sahab's boots, iron his shirts, put out water for his shave. While sweeping and dusting she would run her hands with wonder and amazement at all the beautiful things that Sahab had brought back from Paris. His violin is kept on top of the wardrobe. The first time Tarabai had cleaned the bedroom, she had run her fingers over the violin for a long time. But two days ago, when she had been dusting the violin with utmost care and delicacy as was her norm, the usually mild-mannered and soft-spoken Sahab had entered the room and shouted at her. 'Why have you touched the violin?' he had thundered, and snatching it away from her hands, slammed it back on top of the wardrobe. Poor Tarabai was terrified. Tears came to her eyes. Somewhat ashamed, Sahab had gone out to the balcony where Begum Sahab was drinking tea.

Ordinarily, Begum Sahab's mornings are spent at the hairdresser's and the beauty salon. Manicure, pedicure, massage, facial, sauna bath ... Countless saris, each more beautiful than the other, dozens of colourful bottles filled with perfumes, boxes of attar, and cupboards full of jewellery. But Tarabai thinks that while God has given Begum Sahab wealth, honour and a good-looking husband, the only thing He had been miserly with is a pretty face.

It is said that Sahab was famous in Begum Sahab's social circle precisely because of his good looks, but Begum Sahab has put all sorts of restrictions on him since they have got married. She calls him several times when he goes to office. When he goes out on his own in the evenings, she knows exactly where he's going, and calls to check on him. When the two of them go out together to parties she keeps a sharp eye on him so that he dare not so much as look at another girl. Sahab has gladly accepted all these rules and restrictions because Begum Sahab is extremely wealthy, and Sahab's job too was arranged by his wealthy father-in-law. Before his marriage, Sahab was quite poor and had gone to France on a scholarship to study engineering. Upon his return, he could not find employment and was wandering about dejectedly when Begum Sahab's family had lassoed him. Strange are the ways of the high and mighty!

Tarabai heard these stories from the cook, sweeper, and other servants in the flat, and her eyes would fly wide open with amazement.

Khurshid Alam was a good man and a fine violin player, but since his marriage he had become so lost in his wife's love that he had not touched the instrument. That was also because Almaas Begum had a deep-seated hatred for the violin. Khurshid Alam felt beholden to his wife because his marriage had radically changed his life. Gratitude is such a thing that one can willingly sacrifice music for it.

Khurshid Alam used to live in a decrepit old building and had spent years wandering about the city's streets. Now, he lived like a millionaire on Cumballa Hill. Pecuniary well-being is possibly the most important thing for a man.

Khurshid Alam will never play the violin again.

It was barely a year and a half ago when Almaas was staying at the palatial mansion of her wealthy father in Malabar Hill. She was doing social work. Given her advancing years, she had nearly given up hope of getting married when she met Khurshid Alam at a dinner party. Her aunt, Begum Usmani, who had seen the world and its ways, sensed a possibility and made enquiries with all due diligence: the 'boy' was from UP, had returned from Europe, and was looking for a job, but was not ready for marriage because he had left a girl behind in France and was awaiting her return. Begum Usmani instantly set to work on his behalf. Almaas's father appointed Khurshid Alam in one of his firms at a monthly salary of fifteen hundred rupees. Then he invited Khurshid Alam home, and the meetings with Almaas began to take place. Still, the 'boy' showed no particular interest in the 'girl'. He would perforce have to spend time at her home when he returned from his office. Tired of her shallow and superficial conversation, he would take refuge in the scenic balcony facing the sea.

He would think that one day Piroja's ship would dock at this sea and she would step off it. She would have come back with him, but her work had not finished in Paris. But her ship had sailed beyond the shore and he would keep gazing at the horizon as he bent over the railing of the balcony. At such times, Almaas would appear from the room and placing a hand on his would ask cheerfully, 'What are you thinking about?' And he would become abashed.

After dinner, he would talk to Almaas's father about national politics and high finance. Exhausted, he would reach his home, take out the violin and play tunes on it, the same tunes he had played when he had been with Piroja in Paris. They used to write to each other every third day. In his last letter, he had told her that he had got an excellent job in Bombay. He had made no mention of the frightening suspicions that came with the job.

A year passed, and he showed no signs of wanting to marry Almaas. Finally, Begum Usmani decided that she must speak directly, and clearly, with him. But just then, a telegram came from Pratapgarh informing Khurshid Alam of the sudden illness of his father, and he set out for his 'native' place. Khurshid Alam had been in Pratapgarh for barely a few days when Almaas, who had grown weary of expecting any proposal of marriage from him, went to the Taj Mahal Hotel to hear a concert by a German pianist. As always, there was a crowd of elderly Parsi men and women in the Crystal Room, and a young Parsi woman with beautiful eyes was going about distributing the concert's programme. A common acquaintance introduced Almaas to the young woman.

As was her wont, Almaas examined the unknown girl with a highly critical and sharp gaze. She was extremely good-looking.

'What was the name Mrs Rustomji mentioned for you?' Almaas enquired with obvious interest.

'Piroja Dastur,' the girl answered simply.

'I haven't seen you at any concert before.'

'I have just returned from Paris after seven years.'

'Seven years in Paris? Then you must be speaking French very fluently!' Almaas said with some displeasure.

'Yes, indeed.' Piroja laughed.

By now, some of the special guests were moving towards the lounge with the German pianist. Piroja excused herself and went across to an English lady with whom she soon got engrossed in a very technical conversation on the musical prowess of the German pianist. But Almaas bumped into her again when both were in the lounge.

'There's such a crush for the tea; come, let's sit here,' Piroja smiled and said to Almaas. They sat down at a table set against a window, facing each other.

'You seem to be an expert in music,' Almaas began a bit gruffly, for she could not stand beautiful and young women.

'Yes, I had gone to Paris for higher studies in piano.'

A warning bell went off somewhere in the far distance in Almaas's head. Casting a glance towards the clear and extremely blue waters of the sea, she said with an artless charm and seeming casualness, 'How interesting! We have a piano at home; why don't you come by one day and play something for us?'

'Sure,' Piroja answered cheerfully.

'What's your plan for Saturday? I am having a party and I know my friends will be happy to meet you.'

'I would love to come ... Thank you!'

'Where do you stay, Piroja?'

Piroja mentioned an alley in Tardeo. Almaas drew a breath of relief; Tardeo was inhabited by down-at-heel impoverished Parsi families.

'I live with my uncle; my father has passed away. I have no brothers or sisters. My uncle has raised me. He has no children of his own. He works as a clerk in a bank,' Piroja went on speaking simply.

Then, after a few desultory remarks about this and that, she looked towards the sea and said, 'It's so strange! Last week, when my ship was approaching the harbour, I was saying to myself that I am returning to Bombay like a stranger after seven years. It's a cruel city, Almaas, as you no doubt know. It's so hard to make true friends here. But look at my good fortune. I have met you!

Almaas nodded with every indication of empathy.

A hushed murmur came from the lounge. After a few moments of silence, Almaas asked, 'How did you go to Paris?'

'I got a scholarship. After my degree in piano, I got a research assignment for a few years. I was very happy there, but here, my uncle was all alone. My uncle and aunt are both very old; in fact, my aunt is almost deaf. I came back because of them, and then there's also—'

'Hello, Almaas, you are sitting here. Mrs Mulgaonkar is asking for you,' a lady said as she approached their table.

Piroja's sentence was left unfinished. Almaas took her leave saying she would send her car over on Saturday at 11 a.m. to fetch her and disappeared in the crowd of milling guests.

Piroja reached Almaas's home on Saturday where a hen party was in full flow. The records of the Beatles were being played. A few girls, who had taken part in a fashion show a few days ago, were discussing it loudly. All these girls, whose mother tongue was Urdu, Hindi, Gujarati or Marathi, were speaking in English and nothing but English. They were all dressed in extremely tight pants. For a moment it seemed to Piroja that she had not quite returned to India yet. Having lived in Europe for many years, she had understood how sad and disappointed the Europeans were at the sight of these West-obsessed Indian women instead of the living images of Ajanta they hoped to see. And so, when she lived in Paris and in Rome, Piroja took great pride in her typically Indian style and appearance.

Tired of these fake American girls, Piroja went and stood in the balcony. Ahead of her lay the sea, and on one side the jungle surrounding the Tower of Silence. She noted with alarm the vultures and crows circling high above the jungle. A dense, impenetrable silence lay beneath. Frightened, she stepped back into the room that was resounding with the sounds of life and sat down on a sofa.

A grand piano was placed in one corner of the room, perhaps to serve as a status symbol. The girls were playing songs on the radiogram and the heart-tugging sound of a guitar filled the room. Harry Belafonte's 'Jamaica Farewell' was playing:

Down the way where the nights are gay  
And the sun shines daily on the mountaintop  
I took a trip on a sailing ship  
And when I reached Jamaica I made a stop

But I'm sad to say I'm on my way
Won't be back for many a day
My heart is down, my head is turning around
I had to leave a little girl in Kingston town…

Almaas went and quietly stood in the balcony. When the song ended she went up to Piroja and said, 'We are such Philistines; a master pianist is here and we are playing records! Come on … get up!'

Smiling, Piroja sat down on the piano stool.

'What shall I play? I only know classical music.'

'Oh! … No pop?' the girls let out a collective cry. 'All right … at least play the tune of some Indian film song…'

'I don't know any film songs though, yes, I know a ghazal that someone, someone had…' and she stopped in embarrassment.

'Ghazal! Oh, I love poetry!' a Muslim girl, whose parents were Urdu speakers, cried out in a patronizing manner.

Piroja ran her fingers over the keys and a strange smile fluttered on her lips. Slowly, gently, she began to play an absolutely heart-tugging tune.

'Sing along, sing along!' the girls called out.

'I can't sing; in any case, my Urdu pronunciation is terrible.'

'All right, then, tell us the words, we will sing!'

'It goes like this:

*Tu saamne hai apne bata ke tu kahaan hai*
*Kis tarah tujh ko dekhun nazzara darmiyan hai*

Some of the girls began to sing along: '*Nazzara darmiyan hai … Nazzara darmiyan hai!*'

The ghazal ended, and there was a round of applause.

'Now play a Western piece,' a girl requested.

'Shall I play "The Maiden's Fancy" by Chopin? My fiancé and I used to play this composition together in Paris; he would accompany me on the violin.'

'Is your fiancé a musician too?' one of the girls asked.

'Not a professional; only an amateur,' Piroja answered, and became engrossed in the melody she was playing.

Over the next few weeks, Almaas forged a strong friendship with Piroja. During this time, Piroja found a job teaching piano in a convent college that was supposed to open after the vacations. She also found a tuition to teach piano, thrice a week, to the ten-year-old daughter of an American. The American had recently lost his wife and had come on a tour of India, with his children, to distract himself from his grief. He was staying at the Sun and Sand Hotel in Juhu. It was a fair distance from Tardeo to Juhu, but the American had promised a handsome fee to Piroja; moreover, he had met her with great warmth and kindness.

Piroja was rather pleased with her life. What's more, Khurshid was expected back from his home in a few days. Piroja hadn't told him about getting the job and the tuition so soon after her return; she wanted to surprise him with the good news.

One day, as Piroja was strolling with Almaas in the garden of her palatial house, Almaas asked her suddenly as they approached a fountain, 'Where did you learn that ghazal from?'

'Oh, that? … In Paris…'

'Oh, in Paris? How interesting? Who taught you?'

'My fiancé.'

'Oh, Piroja, you never told me you are engaged!'

'He is from your community…'

'Oh! Really?' Almaas sat down at the rim of the fountain.

'My father and grandfather were very strict, but my uncle is very liberal; he has given his permission.'

'So what's the young man's name?'

Names can be a funny business. Khurshid Alam had fallen in love with her narcissus-like beautiful eyes the very first time he had seen them. When he had met Piroja for the first time at a function at the Indian embassy in Paris, and someone had introduced him to her telling him her name was Piroja, he had remarked mischievously, 'But your name should have been Nargis!'[1]

Piroja had replied, 'Nargeesh? That's my aunt's name!'

'*Lahaoul willa quwwat…*'[2] Khurshid Alam had replied spontaneously, as though he had known her for a long time. 'Nargeesh, Khurshet, Piroja … you people have truly ruined these beautiful Persian names! Do you mind if I call you Firoza?'

'Certainly not,' Piroja had replied with a laugh.

One day, while strolling by the river, he had said to her, 'These brave eyes of yours, these eloquent eyes … these eyes that shine like fireflies, these jewel-bright eyes, these eyes that are like sun-

1 Nargis means narcissus; it's a popular name for girls among Muslims. Among Parsis, it's pronounced and spelt slightly differently, as 'Nargeesh'. In Urdu poetry and literary culture, the nargis flower is a metaphor for a woman with beautiful eyes.

2 A verse in Arabic from the Holy Quran used variously to express disapproval, dissatisfaction or even disgust; loosely translated it means, 'I turn my face from Evil'.

dappled light and glimmering rain, these twin narcissus flowers that have become transformed into your eyes.'

'I asked you ... what's the gentleman's name?'

Piroja was startled by Almaas's sharp voice. 'Khurshet Alam,' Piroja answered.

When she raised her worried glance after a few moments of complete silence, she found that Almaas, dressed in a black sari with a hand resting on her waist and standing like a dark camel in front of her, was saying, 'What a strange coincidence, Piroja dear! My fiancé's name is also Khurshid Alam. He, too, plays the violin, and he, too, has recently returned from Paris. These days, he has gone to his hometown to meet his family.'

Lightning streaked across the August sky, but no one noticed that the clap of thunder fell on Piroja. For some time, she sat motionless. Then, she turned her gaze towards the palatial mansion and visualized her tiny, dilapidated flat. Lightning flashed once again and illuminated this scene at Malabar Hill. In the blink of an eye, Piroja understood everything. And also why Khurshid Alam had not mentioned Almaas in any of his recent letters, or why he had been avoiding the subject of marriage in his letters lately. She got to her feet gently and said softly, 'All right then, Almaas, congratulations on the engagement. Khuda Hafiz!'

'Are you going, Piroja? Wait! My car will drop you. Driver...' Almaas called out languidly.

'No, Almaas, thank you,' she nearly ran out of the gate. A bus had just come to a halt across the road. She quickly crossed the road and sat down in the bus.

Almaas stood near the fountain and kept looking towards the gate. The fierce downpour had bent the palm trees.

⁂

Three days after this incident, Almaas's father received a letter from Khurshid Alam in which he requested an extension of his leave due to the severity of his father's illness. He omitted to write that his dear father, a devout Muslim, was virtually at death's door because of the shock of the news that his only son was hoping to marry a Parsi woman instead of a good Muslim girl from a fabulously rich family.

It was evident from Khurshid Alam's letter that he was greatly troubled. In response, Almaas wrote to him herself:

> Stay there for as long as you wish. Daddy doesn't think of you as an outsider. We are all with you in this difficult time. Why don't you bring Abba miyan here for better treatment?
>
> By the way, I had gone swimming to the Sun and Sand Hotel yesterday; there I met a very interesting Parsi woman, a certain Miss Piroja, who plays the piano and has only recently returned from Paris. She is possibly the girlfriend of some American with whom she is staying at the Sun and Sand. I am mentioning her to you because possibly you may have met her in Paris…
>
> Anyhow, please come back with Abba miyan at the earliest so that a room can be reserved for him at the Breach Candy Hospital.
>
> Yours sincerely,
> Almaas

As evening fell, a taxi came and halted beside a decrepit building in Tardeo, and Khurshid Alam stepped out. He took out a notebook, confirmed the address, then set foot on the stairs leading to the veranda abutting the road. In front of him, the chowk[3] that had been drawn with limestone powder on the doorframe in the morning was still in place. Inside, in the semi-dark room, an elderly Parsi man dressed in grimy white pants and wearing a round white cap on his head, was seated beside a window, mumbling prayers under his breath. A shabby chair stood on one side. A table was covered with a colourful waxcloth and a large portrait of Zarathustra hung on the wall. The room reeked of coconut and fish. An elderly Parsi woman, dressed in a red georgette sari and with her hair covered in a kerchief, emerged from an inner room, her head moving up and down as though with a palsy.

'Is Miss Piroja Dastur here?'

'Piroja?' the woman asked, looking at Khurshid Alam with her misty eyes.

'Has she shifted to the Sun and Sand Hotel?'

The deaf, old woman nodded.

'With … whom…?' Khurshid Alam stuttered.

---

3 A reference to the decorative patterns (also called rangoli) the Parsi community learnt from their Maharashtrian and Gujarati neighbours and is now a common feature in typical Parsi homes; it is usually made from white limestone powder or colourful powders, and is supposed to bring good luck to the household.

The old woman went in and returned with a visiting card that she handed to Khurshid Alam; a foreigner's name was written on it.

'Are you Mr Khorshet Alam? Piroja had said that you might be coming here looking for her and that I must instantly call her and tell you where she has gone.' And she pulled out a twenty-five-paisa coin from the pocket of her blouse.

Khurshid Alam looked at her in amazement.

'You don't have any objection to this state of affairs?'

The deaf old woman shook her head in the negative. 'We are poor people, and when that American…' Suddenly she realized that she had not invited the guest inside. She bent a little from the waist and said, 'Come inside.'

Khurshid Alam stood astonished for a moment then turned around and got into the taxi.

'Bye-bye,' the old woman waved her hand.

The old man finished his prayer and leapt outside, but the taxi had whizzed off.

There was such a terrible downpour on the day of Almaas and Khurshid Alam's engagement party that everything was drenched in rain. Just before dinner it stopped for a bit. Khurshid Alam and Almaas's father's friend, Dr Siddiqui, who had recently been posted here, went and stood in the balcony. The stillness of the Towers of Silence lay coiled a short distance away. Inside, the drawing room echoed with laughter, and the candelabra placed on the grand piano glimmered with lit candles. It was an extremely romantic and opulent setting.

Suddenly, the phone kept in the gallery rang. A servant came and said, 'There is a phone call for Khurshid Sahab.'

Dressed in her bridal finery, Almaas leapt to answer it. A harried-sounding nurse from a local hospital was asking, 'Is Mr Khurshid Alam there?'

'Why do you need to speak to him?' Almaas asked sternly.

'Miss Piroja Dastur has been admitted here for a month. She's been extremely sick. Today, her condition is very delicate. She's asking if Mr Alam can come and see her for a few minutes...'

'Mr Alam is not here.'

'Are you sure?'

'Yes, I am sure,' Almaas thundered. 'Do you think I am lying?' Quickly, she disconnected the line.

Two hours later, the phone rang again.

'Dr Siddiqui, there's a call for you,' someone called out from the gallery. 'You are being called to the hospital urgently.'

Dr Siddiqui went to answer the phone. Then he called out to Almaas, 'Excuse me, my dear, I'll have to run.'

Almaas walked with him till the door. 'We are definitely going to Poona tomorrow for the weekend.'

'Yes, definitely, definitely ... Good night!' Dr Siddiqui said as he left.

Having recovered fully after his stay at the Breach Candy Hospital, Khurshid Alam's father has gone back home to Pratapgarh. The flat at Cumballa Hill, which the bride has received in her dower, is still being readied. So, the newly-wed groom is staying in the bride's home. Often, before leaving for office in the morning, he goes and stands in the balcony. Down below in the jungle, a twisting-winding road snakes up to the Tower of Silence. White-clad Parsi mourners holding each other's hands with white handkerchiefs can be seeing walking up the hill in a single row carrying a corpse on a bier. Vultures and crows sit patiently on the trees. A sea of happy humanity ebbs and flows outside the gates of the Tower of Silence, intent upon travelling to interesting cities.

She had once written in a letter: 'There are thousands of eyes in the mind; there's only one eye in the heart. When love ends, all of life ends.'

The wave that rose in the sea would have spent itself in a moment; the cloud that crossed the sky would have disappeared from sight. When she died, how had the vultures and crows welcomed her? When her spirit left her body at the hospital on that stormy night and reached the skies, would another spirit have asked her: 'Who are you?' And she might have answered: 'I don't know; I died only yesterday.'

Where would her spirit have travelled by now? Dead people travel so far!

Tarabai looks at everything in her Sahab's house with bright, wondering eyes. She looks at Almaas, too, with wonder and amazement. Almaas Begum is expecting. Soon, Tarabai's work is going to double. This morning itself, the eye specialist Dr Siddiqui had come. When Tarabai had brought tea for him this morning, he had looked startled and asked happily, 'Arre, Tarabai, is it you?'

'Yes, Sahab,' Tarabai had answered shyly.

'Can you see everything clearly now?'

'Yes, Doctorji, I can.'

'Good,' and then he turned to address Mrs and Mr Khurshid Alam. 'This girl was blinded at the age of ten. Fortunately, her blindness proved to be temporary. Do you remember, Almaas, I had to leave midway on the night of your engagement party and rush to my hospital? A lady by the name of Miss Piroja Dastur died there that night. She had donated her eyes to the eye bank shortly before she passed away. I was called to harvest her eyes as soon as she died. She had the most beautiful narcissus-like eyes. God knows who she was, that poor thing! A deaf old Parsi woman stood by her bedside crying … It was a hauntingly poignant scene … Anyhow, a few days later, this Tarabai was brought to me by her uncle; some doctor had told him that blindness can be cured with a new corneal transplant. I fitted her eyes with Miss Dastur's corneas. Now look at her eyes shining like stars! Truly, medical science is showing us miracles every day!' Dr Siddiqui finished speaking and lit a cigarette in a leisurely fashion. But Almaas Begum's face suddenly turned white. Khurshid Alam got to his feet shakily and tottered to his room, feeling his way with his hands like a blind man.

Tarabai saw his state and ran towards him. Sahab turned and looked at her like a madman. Tarabai could not understand anything. So she ran to the kitchen and started scrubbing the dishes.

In the distance, the vultures and crows were circling the Tower of Silence.

*Kaaga sab tan khaiyyo, chun chun khaiyyo maas*
*Dui naina mat khaiyyo piya milan ki aas*

Eat every part, pick the body clean, O crow
Just don't eat the two eyes filled with hope of meeting the beloved.

# THE CIRCUMCISION OF KHALID

## *Ghazanfar*

THE LONG-DELAYED FUNCTION was finally taking place.[1] A date, one that suited everyone, had been fixed. The khala and khalu from Pakistan had arrived, as had the mamu and mumani from Arabia.

1 The circumcision, or removal of foreskin from the penis, is ideally performed on the eighth day after the birth of a male child, according to Islamic practice. When not performed on the eighth day and done later, as here, it marks an important rite of passage into adulthood. In either case, the occasion is marked with festivity and rejoicing, with feasting for the extended family and neighbours. In many parts of the Muslim world, the simple operation is still performed by a barber when it is not being done by doctors in a hospital.

The house was full of guests, and glimmering. The walls and doors glistened with a fresh coat of paint. The roofs had been turned into a garden, festooned as they were with brightly coloured paper leaves and flowers. The floors of the rooms sparkled like mirrors. Shimmering moon-white sheets were spread in the courtyard over clean rugs and carpets.

In the veranda outside, large deghs simmered over fires. The fragrance of basmati rice wafted from pots of biryani. The aroma of garam masala wafted out from the degh of qorma and floated far and wide.

Gradually, the women from the neighbourhood began to gather in the courtyard. The clamour of children increased.

Multicoloured dresses created a riot of colour. The soft tinkling of gold and silver jewellery could be heard. Scents from a variety of perfumes permeated the air; their heady fragrance began to fill the senses. Shafts of light emanated from beautifully made-up faces, with sparkling eye shadow glimmering from eyelids. Peals of laughter broke out from red-tinged lips. Colour, radiance and fragrance – all three were suffused in that milieu. The glimmering house sparkled.

Abbu and Ammi were feeling utterly happy, as though every manner of delight had gathered around their feet. Their hearts were suffused with eagerness and enthusiasm. Their eyes were brimming with tears of joy because their son, the apple of their eyes, was about to fulfil the sacred rite that goes back to the time of Abraham. Their faces gleamed with a radiance because their dearest son was about to fulfil his glorious obligation as a Muslim. Their breathing was quick and rapid because their long-nurtured aspiration was finally coming true.

The festivities were reaching their zenith.

The guests came out of the rooms and from the veranda to gather in the courtyard. The people sitting on the white sheets stood up. A large mortar was placed in the middle of the floor.[2] The mortar was covered with a floral-patterned sheet. A sehra made of freshly plucked flowers, to be tied around the boy's head, was kept ready. An embroidered soft cotton kurta was taken out of its wrappings.

The elderly barber opened his small satchel. He took out his razor and laid out his forceps. Then he opened the little packet of ash that he would use instead of sterilizing liquid.

Khalid was called out but he was nowhere to be found. The children were asked about his whereabouts, but everyone answered in the negative. Abbu-Ammi became steadily more worried. A search was launched. After having looked all over the house, Abbu and I finally reached the small, dark storeroom that was used to keep all sorts of discarded rubbish. In the light of the torch, we saw Khalid crouching at the far end of the room, looking like a chicken that had been made to run for a very long time.

'Khalid, my son, here you are, and everyone has been waiting for you for so long. Come on, let's go. Your Ammi is getting worried.'

'No, Abbu, I won't get the circumcision done,' Khalid said, crumpling up his face.

The news of his circumcision had been hidden from Khalid, but possibly someone had told him about it.

---

2 As the story will later reveal, the boy is balanced atop the mortar. Balancing one who is about to undergo a circumcision on a mortar allows the barber to perform the ritual effectively and the hollow of the mortar can collect any blood or other run-off.

'All right, don't get it done, but come out,' Abbu tried to cajole him lovingly. But Khalid kept sitting, stuck to the wall, as though the wall had captured him like powerful magnet. We tried to prise one of his hands free and pull him out, but his other hand went and got stuck to the wall as though it were a snake whose head had gone inside a pit and only its tail was left in our hands. God knows how that little boy had found such strength! After a great deal of effort and much struggle, we managed to pull him out of the storeroom.

'Ammi! Ammi! I won't get the circumcision done,' he wailed. There were tears in his eyes.

'All right, don't. But at least wear this nice new kurta. See, all the other children are wearing new clothes. And look! What a nice sehra this is! It will look so fine on your head.[3] You will look like a bridegroom when you tie it. Everyone has come to see you dressed as a groom. You will get married too!'

'You are lying, Ammi! I know everything! I will not wear the kurta. I will not tie the sehra!'

'See … I have got such a lot of money for you,' said Abbu, scattering a bundle of crackling ten-rupee notes in front of Khalid.

The eyes of the children standing nearby gleamed.

'See, what I have got for you?' the Pakistani khalu opened a box of imported toffees.

The children gathered nearby licked their lips.

---

3 A sehra or veil of tinsel and flowers is usually tied around the head of the bride and groom at the time of marriage, to hide their face till the time of the nikah. But because the circumcision ceremony, known as khatna, is also a rite of passage into manhood, in some homes the little boys are dressed up like grooms.

The mamu who had come from Arabia stepped forward and said, 'See, Khalid, this car is for you. It moves without being wound up…' And at the sound of a clap, the car began to dash about here and there.

But Khalid's eyes were unseeing. They remained still and stricken with fear, like an animal that had spotted the hunter.

Abbu, Ammi, Khalu, Mamu grew tired after making offerings of love, money, toffees, a car. But Khalid wouldn't budge an inch.

Annoyed, Abbu finally resorted to the use of force. He opened Khalid's pants and tried to slide them down, but Khalid held on to the two ends of his pants with both his hands. Along with the tears from his eyes, the sound of crying began to escape from his lips. Khalid's tears made Ammi's eyes wet. 'Don't cry, my darling, don't cry! If you don't want it, we won't force you. We won't have your circumcision done.' Ammi consoled Khalid in a choked voice and dabbed his tears with her aanchal.

For some time, Ammi remained silent. Then, running her hand over Khalid's head, she said, 'Last year, at your phuphi's house when your cousin was getting his circumcision done, you were very insistent that you wanted it too. What has happened to you today? Why have you become such a coward? You are a very brave boy. You had got a surgery done without any fear. This won't cause you any pain, you know.'

'I am not scared of getting the circumcision, Ammi.'

'Then?'

'Abbu, one day you had said that goons kill those who have had a circumcision.'

Khalid's sentence struck Abbu and all the others nearby like a bolt of lightning. They felt as though their tongues were paralysed.

The glimmering, glistening scenario faded and fell silent. The smiles wilted. The fingers of the little boys reached their pyjamas.

Ghastly scenes of search-and-find operations rose before their eyes. Bodies stripped naked. Knives thrust into chests.

Colour faded from the festivities. A cloud of dust swirled over the bright light. Happiness scattered and fled.

The barber's razor became dull. Water was thrown over the ash.

In an attempt to lighten the atmosphere, the khalu from Pakistan addressed Khalid: 'Khalid my son, do you know what will happen if you don't get circumcised? Seeing you are not circumcised, the circumcised goons will kill you.'

'Is that true, Abbu?' Khalid was shaking from head to toe.

'Yes, my son, your khalu is telling the truth.'

'All right then, get my circumcision done.' And the open ends of his pants slipped from his hands. The pants slid below his hips. Khalid was ready for the circumcision.

Despite his agreement, no one tied a sehra around his head. No hand was raised to dress him in the new kurta.

When the painful silence became unbearable, the Pakistani khalu stepped forward and seated Khalid on the mortar.

The ceremony began. But no one dropped any money into the barber's tray. The barber, too, did not make any such demands.

Silently, he filled the ash under the foreskin, tightened the straps, adjusted the strip of skin in the forceps, and placed a quivering razor over it. He looked as though he was about to cut someone's neck, not perform a circumcision.

# A RAT'S DEATH

## *Zakia Mashhadi*

IT MUST HAVE been the fourth time that Mishrji had come by.

'Tell me clearly: will you go or not? If you are ready, I will write down your name. I don't want to keep asking you. I won't come again. We have to leave day after tomorrow.'

Dhena showed his yellow teeth and began to scratch his head. The wheat harvest had begun. The crop had been removed from most of the fields. Musahar and Chamar[1] boys could be seen

1 Musahar belong to a Dalit community found in the eastern Gangetic plain and the Terai. Their name literally means 'rat eater' due to their main occupation being catching rats, and eating them, such being their destitution. Due to their occupation and the fact that they eat the rats they catch, they occupy the lowest rung in the socio-economic

picking the fallen grain from the fields. Pheeku had collected a basketful; it must have weighed at least half a ser. Naturally, he was very pleased. If only he were to get some more grain ... His family had not eaten rotis to their hearts' content for God knows how long. A few days ago, he had found a wild rabbit – it was enough to fill a pot. But it wasn't so every day. Some days, he couldn't find even rats – and two or three rats were not enough. His two sons seemed to have a jinn in their stomach. Amma was old but she ate just the same as everyone else. And, on top of everything else, she had become greedy. One day, she said she wanted a little oil. They barely had money to buy salt; from where was one to get oil and masalas? At best they could boil some snails and roast rats that had been caught from the forest and cooked over dry twigs. His wife was the only person who never ever complained. Stone-faced, she would go about her chores, busy all day long collecting fuel for the fire that was forever raging in their stomachs.

'You will get eight rupees, and also sherbet and puris with sabzi,' Mishrji had said as he was leaving.

A banquet was conjured up in Dhena's mind at these words: puri, sabzi and sherbet. A banquet would be conjured up in his mind every time Mishrji came. But Dhena was scared of the city; so much so that his fear would eclipse the greed for this manna from heaven. He had heard that the roads in the city were so wide that one could go crazy just crossing them from one side to the

---

and caste pyramid. Chamar is also a Dalit community, classified as a scheduled caste under modern India's system of affirmative action, they traditionally dealt with leather and the handling of skins of dead animals.

other, and the lights so bright as though lightning were coursing through the skies! Large and terrifying-looking cars would be dashing about. God knows how people lived there! Don't they die of terror?

'How do people live here? They are subhuman beings!' Once, a woman had said this about Dhena's village. A team had come from the Punjab Agricultural Institute to conduct research on rats and other rodents, and had somehow stumbled into Dhena's remote village. There were two women too. Two women along with eight men, looking like boys with neither a veil over their head nor modesty in their gaze! Dhena gaped at them. A swarm of naked, dark-skinned children from the village and a few youths trailed the jeep. For it was seldom that one saw such strange marvels in their village. Their mouths open, each one of them bore an expression of utter stupidity.

'So many villages and so desolate! I am feeling suffocated, as though someone has trapped me in a cage,' one of the women said. Dhena thought she was slightly 'off'. For one thing, she was dressed like a man despite being a woman and her hair was cut short. And on top of that, she was making these peculiar pronouncements. She was in an open land stretching from here to there; there was an open sky above too. Yet she was feeling suffocated! The world is full of strange people! Their bellies are full. They are dressed from head to toe. Who gives them so much? Dhena was going mad searching for these answers.

According to the team's report, the population of rats was amazingly low in the area, whereas scores of ratholes could be seen in the fields.

Why were these people talking of rats? Do they, too, eat rats? Dhena gathered his courage and moved ahead. 'Sahab, tell me a way in which we can increase the population of rats.'

'Hundreds of thousands of tonnes of wheat in this country are eaten by rats, and this moron is asking for a way to increase the number of rats!'

'Sir, he eats rats,' someone piped in.

'Our entire village eats rats,' Dhena answered with the utmost simplicity.

'An easy and simple method of rodent control … eat them!' Dr Nafees, the leader of the team, who seldom laughed, could not help laughing out loud.

'The government is spending lakhs of rupees, yet the rats are defying all the propositions of all the teams, consuming all the poisons and inhaling all the toxic fumes, and are still alive.'

'In much the same way that human beings are alive after eating rats.'

'Arre, why are you going on about eating rats? Akhh-thooo…' This time the woman couldn't control her nausea and actually threw up.

What a strange woman she was! If one were to catch fifteen to twenty fat rats and ten to fifteen snails, there would be enough for everyone in Dhena's house to eat one square meal. But what about puri-sabzi?

Dhena's boy Pheeku was ten years old, but he had never eaten puris; he had not even seen them, actually. Nor had he ever drunk sherbet. He would roam around naked. In fact, until two years ago, completely naked! It was only in the past two years that he had begun to tie a piece of cloth around his loins. His wife had walked two and a half kos to go to Mukhiyaji's house to thresh grain. She had single-handedly cleaned and cut two mann worth of jackfruit with her sickle. She had worked non-stop for three days. For this, she had got two full meals each day and a coarse cotton dhoti. She had torn the dhoti into four pieces. One of those pieces had gone to Pheeku. A stomach full of rice twice a day for three whole days! Upon her return when she told people about it, everyone got a gleam in their eye. An acute sense of envy pierced deep into Dhena's soul. Unfortunately, Mukhiyaji had sent only for his wife; not him or his son. Had he gone, he would have eaten so much that his hunger would have been satisfied for many, many days to come. His wife had told him that five sacks of rice would be cooked for each meal. The storehouse was stacked with dozens of sacks of rice. Rats milled about among them.

'We should have a cat,' the fat cook had said.

'The cat won't eat all the rats. Call Dhena Musahar; he will catch all the rats,' the boy helping the cook had said. And then they had all burst out laughing scornfully.

There was scorn, revulsion and derision in their laughter.

Man has not left anything that cannot be eaten: rats, mice, snakes, monkeys, dogs, goats, pigs, cows, camels. And the funny thing is that those who eat goats hate those who eat cows. And those who eat cows refer to those they hate as pig-eaters! And he who was mocking Dhena was an Adivasi who ate both cows and pigs. Once, while making fun of Dhena, he had said, 'Oh you, you eater of rats!' How easy it is to hate someone or consider them inferior! It is all about what one eats!

Now, if Dhena were to get puri-sabzi, why would he eat rats? Forget puri-sabzi, if only he could get roti-chutney, roasted chilli and rice, and if nothing else, a few drops of mustard oil and salt and a stomach full of rice. He would say yes the next time Mishrji came.

When Dhena agreed to go, Mishrji gave him thick chappals made out of rubber tyres. He had to walk a long distance over rough terrain. He would fall on the way if his feet were to get pricked by thorns or stones, or if he were to get blisters. He was also handed a flag. Dhena put the flag to one side and began to examine the chappals, turning them round and round in his hands. For a long time, he wore them in his hands. This sacred object, that had come his way so easily, was worth placing on the head. His feet raised the banner of protest; they were not used to wearing chappals. Black feet, black as the black soil at the bottom of the dry pond and just as parched, with cracks and fissures! These were the first of the many rewards he would get courtesy Mishrji. The chappals now began to eclipse the fear of the city. Thirty-year-old Dhena ran like a child, holding the chappals on his head, to show them to his wife and children.

'Hey you, pick up the flag!' Mishrji shouted.

There were many of them. Like rats driven out of their holes. They made up nearly a half-mile-long procession. Each one was carrying a flag in his hand. By now, the sherbet had reached their bellies. For a long time they had been shouting 'jindabad-jindabad'.[2] After every twenty to twenty-five men, there would be

2 *'Inquilab Zindabad'* (literally meaning 'Long Live the Revolution') is the rallying cry of processionalists and protestors across faiths and ideologies across India. However, as this story unfurls, the idea behind

a worker like Mishrji who would raise the cry of 'inquilab'. Who knew what 'inquilab' meant? Puri-sabzi, sherbet, or simply a fat rat!

Hunger was knocking about Dhena's stomach. God alone knew when they would be fed. Sometimes he would fall silent; sometimes he would shout 'jindabad-jindabad' without waiting to hear 'inquilab'. By now, his voice had dropped a few notches. His feet were used to moving about without any restriction; now they felt weighed down by the tyre chappals. He wanted to take off the chappals and hold them in his hands but the tarred road was blistering hot. The dirt of the village track was never this scorching. Nor had he ever experienced such heat and humidity in his village. He walked along desultorily and despondently. Sometimes, he would fall back from his place in the line.

Suddenly, some loud voices were heard from the head of the procession and a commotion rippled through the crowd. Dhena craned his head to see what was happening. A posse of policemen, with canes aloft, was stopping the procession from moving forward. A rope was cordoned across the road. Petrified, Dhena froze in his position. He was terrified at the very mention of police; they seemed fantastical, unreal figures, like the henchmen of Yamraj, the God of Death, sent to catch people.

Dear God! Had I known, I would never have come! To reassure himself, he looked around on either side but couldn't spot anyone he knew. Some twenty to twenty-five people from Dhena's neighbouring villages had come with him, but they were scattered

---

the slogan is seldom fathomed by those who are hired for trifles to be a part of such processions. Also, this being the Hindi-speaking belt, the 'z' of 'zindabad' is altered to 'j'.

somewhere in that long queue of people. God knows if they were ahead or behind. The commotion had increased at the head of the procession. The place where the police was stopping people from moving ahead was located at a tri-junction. A procession had come from the opposite direction and joined them. The slogan-shouting had picked up tempo, and everyone had come to a standstill.

Dhena stood scratching his head, looking completely lost, as he turned this way and that to scan the faces near him. Some of the people near him seemed far more experienced than him. They had been brought for such processions many times in the past. Stuffed in jeeps, they had even been taken to drop little pieces of paper into boxes.[3] Like donkeys carrying loads of mud and rubble, they would 'carry' political leaders. But Dhena was himself a lump of dirt, a wild creature of the forest, a rat that had emerged from his burrow.

'We have to remain steadfast,' the leaders had instructed the workers. 'Never mind if there is a lathi-charge.[4] We will not let it go any further. We will never let it get to the stage of firing. In fact, let there be a lathi-charge or firing of tear-gas shells. Or else, how will it reach the newspapers and how will people find out about the protest?'

---

3 The original says '*parchi girane ke liye*', literally meaning 'to drop little pieces of paper'. Here, it refers to vote fixing or vote tampering by bogus voting at manual ballot boxes.

4 A 'lathi-charge' is a peculiarly Indian expression; I have chosen to retain it in the translation. It means the use of lathis (batons) by the police to disperse a crowd. Usually, police forces are instructed to first use lathis and only then resort to other forms of crowd control, such as water cannons, tear gas, rubber pellets and, in the last resort, firing in the air.

The police did a mild lathi-charge. Commotion broke out among the first few rows of the procession. Like waves rippling on the surface of water, the tumult travelled down the length of the procession. Dhena was already distracted and terrified by hunger, thirst, heat, and the faces of the policemen. Even the thought of the eight rupees he would get at the end of it all was not enough to bring him any comfort. His wife's face swam before his eyes, and the faces of his two young boys. And his mother's naked, shrivelled, pendulous breasts, as well as his father's soot-black face lined with wrinkles. Thorn-laden acacia trees and dry, cracked, parched earth. The wind raising little dust devils, the goat grazing at the small hillock, golden sheaves of wheat lying scattered here and there after the crop had been harvested – all these images swam before his eyes. Surely a ser or a ser and a half of wheat would come out of the pickings his wife and sons gleaned from the fields. The wheat would be ground in his home. Once the wheat was ground, rotis would be made.

At that moment, all he wanted was to hide in the aanchal of his stone-faced wife! An intense desire to run away rose in his heart – to run away from here and go to that familiar milieu where he had nothing and yet everything was his own.

Suddenly, the crowd surged. Dhena ran unthinkingly. His brain had stopped functioning. He didn't even realize that running straight ahead would take him further away from the others in the procession and he would not be able to return to his village without Mishrji's help. He didn't have a paisa in his pocket, nor an ounce of sense in his head. Like an unharnessed camel, Dhena had barely run a hundred yards or so when he came under the wheels of a police jeep that was hurtling from the opposite direction.

Order was soon restored in the restive crowd. The stampede was a minor one and was contained without further ado. The news that a man had been killed on the road reached the crowd after a long time. It wasn't clear whether the dead man was a part of the procession or a passer-by. Mishrji handed over the charge of the men he had got from the Musahar community of Satpedwa village to one of his associates, with the task of returning them to their homes. That man didn't bother to find out whether one man was missing or Mishrji had given him an extra eight rupees. He simply pocketed the money and loaded up all the men into a bus. A few people from Dhena's village enquired about him, but others said, 'So many buses are going back that way. He can climb into any one of them.'

Dhena's corpse lay in the government mortuary for three days. When the dead body could not be identified, sixty rupees were released from the government funds to take care of his last rites. After the post-mortem, Dhena, stuffed in a large, coarse cotton bag bearing government markings, was handed over to a Dom for funerary rites.

Rascals! Would they cremate their mothers in sixty rupees! Don't they know the cost of firewood? They know everything. But they think we have a shower of wealth in our house and we can spend money from it on the cremation of unclaimed bodies. Grumbling, Sarju Dom, loaded Dhena's body on a hand cart and trundled it towards the bridge over the Gomti River in the dead of the night. First, he dumped Dhena on to the ground, then he pulled the cloth bag off the body. There was at least a two-and-a-half-metre-long cloth here, and the width too was substantial. If he were to open the stitching along one side, he would get a perfectly fine length of cloth; one could wear it as a dhoti or use it as a chadar. Earlier, it would sell for ten rupees; now one could get fifteen rupees for it. Come, dear sir, in you go into the lap of Mother Gomti. May God bless you! You are a healthy young man. Why did you come here to die? With these words of farewell, Sarju propped Dhena on his feet and then tipped him over the bridge.

Sarju Dom was getting on in years. On top of that, there was the hard work of pushing the cart all the way to the bridge. He couldn't push the body with all his strength; moreover, his angle was all wrong. Instead of toppling straight into the water below, the corpse got caught in the girders of the bridge. Clutching the chadar and the sixty rupees, Sarju went off towards the toddy house.

Early next morning, shortly after the break of dawn, some passing milkmen saw the body caught in the girders of the bridge; then some morning walkers spotted it and then some more. Finally, a small crowd gathered.

'Daily murders! Wanton killings! Where is our society heading?' someone remarked.

'I say, you seem worried at the sight of one corpse! Go to Punjab!' another gentleman chimed in.

'Why not go to neighbouring Bihar? Punjab is far away,' a third voice was heard.

'Yes, as though UP is pure and peaceful!' another person added, looking sternly at the previous speaker who had mentioned Bihar.

The man slunk away. These Biharis were everywhere!

Now, there were only four people left. As it happened, one of them was a Bihari.

'The poor man must have died in police custody,' said a man who had just joined this small group. Two news reporters, too, had arrived, sniffing their way to the spot.

One of them fished out a notebook. The other one laughed out loud.

'You will remain an idiot all your life! First take into consideration the news value of an incident. Leave this for some vernacular rag. They will carry it with the following headline: "A Sensational Murder in Broad Daylight!" Terrorists gunned down thirty to forty people in one single day in Punjab, yet the news appeared in some tiny box in the "States" section of national newspapers. Now, unless at least five hundred to a thousand people die, it makes not the slightest bit of difference to anyone.'

One or two people were more civic-minded than the rest. As they walked on, they informed a constable who was stationed about two hundred yards away. The constable reached the spot, banging his long, stout stick on the ground. He looked closely at the corpse.

'What the hell! This is not a murder. This is a government "disposal". See, see this...' he signalled two respectable-looking persons to come closer. And he threatened two loutish-looking lads to stay away. Then he turned Dhena's body over with the help of his long stick. The corpse had begun to deteriorate by now. There was the gash from the post-mortem, stretching from the chest to the abdomen; it had been closed up with long, coarse stitches. A tag was around the neck like a talisman; it contained some details, probably inscribed by the police and the government doctor.

People stepped back. The crowd dispersed. The constable pushed Dhena's upturned body with his stick. It fell into the river with a splash, but after a few seconds, it bobbed up and began to float in the water. The vultures perched on the trees beside the river looked at each other with meaningful eyes and fluttered their wings. Muttering to himself, the constable spat out loudly and vigorously, then wiped his mouth on his sleeve. 'A stinking corpse first thing in the morning!'

Postscript: Somewhere far, far away, in a remote village in the back of beyond, some people were awaiting the return of their loved one who had gone to get eight rupees, and maybe some leftover puris. And some were busy pulling down the places of worship of others and slitting each other's throats in order to usher in Ram Rajya in the fair land of Hindustan that is akin to paradise.

# THE STONE AGE

*Gulzar*

THE BOMB HAD fallen some distance away, but the walls of the house could not bear the impact of its explosion. After all, they were made of mud. In a matter of moments, they crumbled. His younger sister was buried in the debris and died. The elder sister picked him up and ran; her face unveiled, the smoke in the alley provided a veil. The father held the mother's hand, tucked a bundle of some belongings and a trunk that was always kept packed and ready, and all of them ran away.

He was four years old then.

'Abbu … here … the goras are on that side!'

And he jumped away from his Apa's side. His eyesight was sharp. Coming from the road ahead, a jeep passed by showering bullets along the way.

'Naseer has saved us!'

His sister smothered him with kisses. His mother showered him with love and blessings.

There was a strange sort of glimmer in Naseer's eyes. Like the glint in the eyes of a cheetah. He was getting used to this life in the jungle. Now, even the memory of a home was beginning to fade. They would stay away for two or three months at a stretch, then return briefly. To collect the scattered pots and pans, boxes and bundles, and then flee once again. Dadi was the only one who stayed put, lying in one place, like a bundle of hay.

He was two years old when he had first heard the roar of the aeroplanes and the thunder of bombs. His entire house shook as he clung to his mother's breast and trembled. His mother had tied him to her chest with a sling fashioned out of a wide piece of cloth. She clutched a bundle in one hand and held Bano, his younger sister, in the other. His father had a little trunk tucked under his arm. He was muttering something under his breath as he was dragging his mother to the door, and then said, 'Amma! Try, try a little! Hold Allah's finger and come till the mosque.'

Dadi too was muttering and cursing God knows who: his father or God? Naseer's eyes had been glittering then too. He had seen stars falling from the skies. And suns bursting upon the earth. An innocent thought had crossed his mind even then. 'Why is Allah so terrifying? ... Why does He scare us so?'

Two years is far too short an age, but the eyes ... the eyes can swallow and gobble a great deal during this tender age. And hoard all that they see. To ruminate over later, like camels!

The mosque was filled with the stench of blood. Bleeding hands, knees, shoulders, necks! There were very few people who were whole and intact. For Naseer, this was the 'normal' view of the world. This was the world he had seen from the day he had opened his eyes. This was the world he had grown up in. To see blood on the ground and want to splatter it with his feet was much the same to him as splashing his feet in rainwater.

He heard many new names in the mosque. He knew the names of most of his clansmen. But Russian, American, Bush, Turgenov, firangi, copter, helicopter … these seemed to be names of some other clans. Their jungles must be beyond those hills – from where these helicopters flew in, from where these balls of fire came in to destroy their homes. He hadn't yet forgotten the death of his tiny sister.

'Houses fall down, don't they, Abbu? … Then why do we live in houses?'

He was three years old when he had asked this question. Those days, they had come to stay in a city with pucca houses.

'It rains fire outside, son, because bombs fall,' his father had said.

'Who drops them?'

'They … those white people who come in helicopters.'

'Why do they drop bombs?'

'Because they are our enemies!'

'Are we, too, their enemies?'

'Of course, what else?'

And a year and a half later, he had asked:

'So, can we too drop a bomb on their mountain?'

'We don't have helicopters, son.'

'Then how will we drop them?'

'We have the fidayeen; that's why we have sent our martyrs.'

He didn't understand. The words were becoming difficult … fidayeen! He added another word to his piggybank. He would 'spend' it when he grew up. Though he had fallen silent, he was far from satisfied with such answers. But like flies, these questions would keep buzzing around his face. He would go and sit outside and work on making his slingshot.

He would often remember his Dadi. She had told him many stories during the few months that they had spent in the 'black' mosque in Kandahar.

'The monstrously tall Artful Imposter had taken the fairy and trapped her in a sky-high tower. The fairy lived in one tower and the Artful one in the other. He had trimmed the fairy's wings so she could not even fly away. The twin towers were so tall that no one could reach their tops. When people gathered at the base of the towers, he would pluck one feather off her and let it drop. The people milling about on the ground would run for thousands of miles to catch it.'

'Even the prince?' he had asked.

'Yes, even he was there, but what could he do? He could neither climb up nor fly…'

Suddenly, a coin fell out of the piggybank. He said, as though to himself, 'Why didn't they send the fidayeen?'

By now, he had understood the meaning of fidayeen. Had Dadi been here, he would have told her. He asked his father where she was.

He answered, 'She is with Allah now … He has taken her.'

'Dadi too?' And he fell silent again.

It was hard to tell whether the minaars of the mosque were getting smaller or he was growing taller. He would get up from

Dadi's bundle of rags and climb the steps of the minaar, like a rat scampering out of a sack. He could see the entire city from there. From that vantage point, the city looked like a large brick kiln. Smoke spiralled out from many places. Those must be the bakers' shops. Meat must be cooking there. Kababs being made.

Naseer was growing up very quickly. His clothes kept getting smaller. Dadi would keep finding clothes for him, God knows from where and whose. He had heard the rumble of the tanks from that minaar. The ground would seem to shake when they trundled through the bazaar. They looked like those iron rhinos from Dadi's magical stories, hurtling forward with their snouts raised, spewing fire.

There was another attack. The rhinos surrounded the mosque and set up a siege that lasted days. In the darkness of the night, some people would be let out from the basement of the mosque, like cattle. Crawling on their knees and elbows, they would cross the alley and go across the clear ground. Naseer, too, escaped like this, along with his Ammi and Apa. Abba and Dadi were left behind.

There was another village behind the mountain. Some families found refuge in a stable. There was little noise here. Abba would visit every few days. Once, Abba didn't come for many days. Ammi would fall in prostration and pray. She would always be praying. Her eyes would always be wet with tears. Once, Naseer asked her as he lay on the ground: 'What are you praying for, Ammi?'

'I was asking Allah to keep your father safe, my son.'

Naseer kept lying on the ground and staring at the sky. Then, he asked softly, 'Ammi, whose side is Allah on? Our side, or theirs?'

He turned around. But Ammi had gone.

One night, Naseer tucked his sling in the folds of his salwar and, sniffing his way through the dark, reached the same basement of the mosque. The sight that his eyes beheld numbed him. The mosque had been completely destroyed from inside. There was debris everywhere, and a stink too. As his eyes got accustomed to the darkness, he saw the arms and legs of corpses sticking out from beneath the wreckage. The way to the minaar was blocked with rubble. When morning broke and he moved towards the main gate, he spotted some people. Their nose and face swaddled with cloth, they carried shovels in their hands. Perhaps they had come to clear the rubble. Hiding as best as he could from them, Naseer came out of the mosque. Seeing a crowd of people outside, he quickly climbed into a truck that was parked beside the wall.

An avalanche of dead bodies, their arms and legs missing, and badly mutilated corpses began to be piled into the truck. Naseer crouched in a corner, nearly buried under the mound of dead bodies. He had seen heaps of such half-cut, partly skinned goats, loaded on to carts, being brought to the butcher's shop.

He lay where he was. The truck moved. Who knew which butcher's shop he would be dumped at! During the journey that lasted some hours, it is hard to tell whether he passed out or fell asleep. But when the truck emptied its contents into the maw of a mountain and he fell out, he came to his senses with a start. The truck dumped its human debris into a large pit and went away. Naseer crawled out from under that rubble of dead bodies. A naked rocky mountain rose above him; it was pockmarked with the mouths of caves looking like small, open rat holes. Climbing on all fours, he scrambled up the mountain face like a scared fox and sought refuge in a cave-like crevice.

He could see the human rubble from here. By the evening, the pit had been filled and closed. Naseer stayed there all night. He could hear some human voices in the darkness of the night. Perhaps some people were staying in the caves near him. He could see some eyes prancing about; maybe they belonged to wild rabbits. Searching around him with his hands, Naseer collected some small stones and pebbles. The sling was still tucked in a fold of his salwar. He took it out. He found a small, pointed stone which he began to rub against a bigger stone. He remembered his Dadi.

'In the beginning of time, men made weapons out of stone. They hunted for food and lived in caves. Those clans that had fire would be considered superior to others. They moved to open grounds, travelled and conquered new territories…'

Naseer was preparing a stone weapon by rubbing a small, sharp stone against a bigger stone.

# THE HALTED TRAIN

*Abdus Samad*

THE MOVING TRAIN stopped, suddenly … very suddenly.

It was pitch black outside … with not a trace of light for miles around.

Perhaps it was a dense forest … or a deserted wasteland.

'Why has the train stopped?'

'Has someone pulled the chain?'

'No, perhaps not … Had someone pulled the chain, a guard or someone would have come out to check with a torch.'

'Then…? There isn't an outer signal anywhere here.'

'Stopping the train in this deserted place … What does it mean?'

'Maybe there's something wrong with the track ... This sort of thing is quite common on this line.'

'Anything can happen, brother ... anything is possible. Entire trains have been known to be robbed here after they have been halted with complete nonchalance ... No one will bother.'

'It is the driver and guard's responsibility ... The lives and belongings of so many people are at stake...'

'What can the driver and guard do? The reins of control are with the babu sitting in the control room, the one who can set a train moving on a track as he wishes and stop one when he wants...'

'He must be getting stifled sitting in the control room ... thinking of his wife and children and family. And in his solitude, he must also be thinking of his long-lost love ... After all, what is the poor man to do? ... The rail tracks are spread before him like a chessboard ... and he keeps playing with them.'

'Just imagine ... the sheer number of lives, families, fates, dreams, beliefs, the many pasts and presents that are trapped between this man's fingers. And no one ever talks of changing this system?'

'How can the system be changed? Is it a game? It takes centuries to set up a system and get it going, brother. To talk of pulling it out in minutes when it takes so long to install it in the first place...'

'But we must give it some thought, brother. If not us, it will help our future generations.'

'This is talk for those who live in a dream world. Where is its place in the real, lived world?'

'You mean we should not think about it because it can bring no gain to us personally? Had our forefathers adopted the same attitude, we would never have inherited this system we are now talking about.'

'It would have been good ... very good. Because then we would have had the system of the jungle. In any case, when all systems have to end up going towards the jungle, why not start with the jungle...'

'Surely we cannot negate the importance of the Stone Age. After all, all our streams of thought have emanated from there. And it is only a matter of principle that a thing that has issued forth from a source must go back to its source.'

'Arre, brother, are we going to remain tangled in these pointless arguments or are we going to consider the real problem? The train stopped such a long time ago ... Does anyone know when it will start moving?'

'There's only one thing to be done ... One of us should go and find out why it has stopped.'

'But who will go out?'

'He ... not him ... You ... not you ... Then, him...'

'That means, no one...'

'Wah, such big talk and...'

'The issue is that this is an unknown desolate place, the door of the compartment is shut; we don't know if an escort party is with us or not ... What is waiting for whom outside this closed door, who knows...'

'What are we going to do if we are so scared? ... It is fear that has brought us to this pass...'

'If that is so, why don't you lead the way? The rest of us will follow.'

'That's a good one! No, thank you. I am not especially fond of taking on the role of a leader. I am fine where I am. I will suffer the same fate as everyone else.'

'This is true of all such people in our country who have the capability to think and understand … It is going to become the greatest tragedy of our times…'

'Brothers, for God's sake, do something. The train has been stationary for so long, and no one is doing anything. We are inviting certain death with our blithe, careless behaviour. If there are any train robbers hereabouts, they will surely be alerted by the halted train.'

'My dear good people, does anyone have any weapon of any sort?'

'That's the greatest joke of the day…'

'Five or six robbers come and rob an entire train. Does anyone ever confront them?'

'We have been talking about getting robbed all this time, but has anyone given any thought to the driver who is driving this train at great risk to his own life…'

'That is because we passengers don't even recognize the driver and the guard…'

'What difference does that make? The very basis of our system is…'

'This entire system … this is the root of all evil … Praise the Lord! We are travellers, indeed, but we do not recognize the one who leads the way.'

'What good would it do even if we recognized him? It wouldn't have made any big difference? The difference between him and us would remain in any case…'

'Brother, I am saying it again: instead of all this big talk, we should focus all our attention on finding out why the train stopped and when it will start moving.'

'What a wretched train this is! Not a single person selling tea or peanuts or anything has shown up...'

'Do you know what the time is?'

'But these people are at their jobs 24/7. They are not concerned by the time.'

'These are the people who have the correct news about trains or else there is no public forum for such news. We live in such darkness ... Imagine, there are thousands of people...'

'There is darkness inside, there is darkness outside ... there is darkness everywhere...'

Suddenly, a passenger came huffing and panting from somewhere and collapsed on a seat with a thud. All the talkers fell silent as though struck by lightning.

'Do you know why the train has stopped?' the newcomer asked.

'Perhaps...'

'All wrong! Up ahead someone has removed the fishplate ... A huge accident could have taken place had we...'

By now, this passenger had gained control over his breathlessness. And having transferred the terror from his eyes to the others, he seemed more at peace.

'Oh my God, we have been saved from a huge accident! We have been needlessly cursing the driver, the guard, the control room, the entire system. This is why it is said that without verifying facts one should...'

'Brother, where did you get this confirmed information from?'

'I have just been to see the guard. Don't you know the train is interconnected? I thought I should quell your anxiety…'

'That is very good of you … we are very grateful … Now please also tell us if there is any likelihood of moving any time soon or…'

'Work is in progress. But how can the train move forward until the track is fixed?'

'Anyhow, as long as our lives are safe, all is well. We will reach our destination sooner or later.'

An anxious-looking passenger emerged from the toilet.

'There isn't a drop of water in the toilet…'

'That's terrible news! What are we going to do? Who knows how long we will have to wait…'

'Even if they want to, they can't make any arrangements. Where will they find water in this wilderness?'

'It's possible some people have water, but then they need it when they get thirsty. There are children and old people…'

'Let's solve the issue at hand … We will see about the future later…'

No one mentioned the word 'water'.

'If you are not ready to help each other in this moment of crisis, what can one expect later? … What is the use of all this big talk?'

'Both things are important in their own right … Thirst is as important as one's other needs. Let's not blame anyone. Instead, let's think of a third way…'

'Third way? … As though we have crossed the first and second paths? Where does the question of this third way arise?'

'This is a long argument. No purpose will be served by getting entangled in this. There are many things that one should simply acknowledge and accept. I have accepted ... you have accepted ... That's the end of the matter...'

'Uff! My stomach hurts! For God's sake, someone help me!'

'Brother, a man is groaning in pain right in front of our eyes, and we...'

'What can we do? We are helpless...'

'Brother, you should go to the toilet right now. We will see what we can do in the meanwhile ... If only there was a newspaper or something ... a piece of paper ... anything ... Let's see...'

But nothing was to be found.

Those who had newspapers, hid them, as did those who had sheaves of paper. Though there were scraps of papers used by the peanut seller to sell his peanuts. One man quickly picked these up and handed them to the man groaning in pain, which he grabbed with great alacrity and promptly moved towards the toilet.

'The funeral of humanity is nigh...' muttered the man who had just done the good deed.

'The bier of humanity is travelling on this very train, sir...'

'Don't be sarcastic ... Tell me, should we not have helped this man in distress? He was groaning in pain. Just think: what would have happened? After all, this is not something that one can hold for very long.'

'Come, come, so you have performed a larger good, a general obligation on behalf of all of us ... At least there is one amongst us who is willing to do so. As long as there is one such person amongst us...'

Suddenly, the sound of some people walking outside could be heard. The blinding light from some torches lit the windows of the closed compartment.

Some people had shown the courage to venture out.

'What happened, brother? Why has the train stopped?'

'No one knows … We are still looking…'

Everyone turned to look at the man who had brought along the information about the missing fishplates, but he was nowhere to be found.

'Perhaps he has gone in search of some new information.'

'Some people keep bringing news just to show their importance.'

'At least they are better than us because they are actively engaged…'

'Some people are in the habit of making their faces contort with worry over all sorts of things; it brings them some sense of contentment.'

'Again, we are getting entangled in other things…'

'Meaning…?'

'Meaning, what the passengers are doing is none of our business; the conduct of those whose responsibility it is to ensure we reach our destination should be our concern.'

'The conduct of both…'

'Why? Why ours? How is it our fault? We are simply travellers … Why has the train stopped? What are we doing in this wilderness? Are we doing anything at all, or…? This situation has been foisted on us. *They* have created the problem. So we should talk about *their* conduct … in fact, condemn *their* conduct.'

'Have they created the problem, or are they, too, a victim of the situation? Let us first decide that.'

'If that was so, why did they not anticipate it? Why did they not look at the reason and the consequence, the cause and the effect? If they are moving with so many people, after all, don't they have a responsibility towards them?'

Suddenly, a commotion was heard at a distance. The windows were quickly pulled down. People began to check the bolts and at least two persons leapt to stand at the doors, prepared for any untoward incident. A peculiar sensation crept through the compartment. People forgot their chatter. The distant voices continued to be heard.

Suddenly, one man laughed out loud. Many angry stares were directed towards him.

'Don't be angry, my brothers. There is no reason to get angry. I am simply laughing at your cowardice.'

'Brother, what you should do is leave us cowards here and step outside to find out what is going on.'

'Why, brother? Why should I do that? I am not a saint or a holy man … nor a prophet sent by God.'

'You were laughing at our cowardice, that's why…'

'It is good that I am simply laughing. That time is not far away when you will be laughing at yourself…'

Suddenly, the closed doors began to be pounded from outside. Terrified, everyone crouched into themselves. The man who had been laughing suddenly leapt to his feet and moved towards the door.

'Stop! … For God's sake, stop him … I knew from the beginning he was up to no good!'

But before anyone could stop him, the man opened the door. Three or four harried-looking men entered the compartment.

'This is too much! We have been pounding the door for so long and you haven't opened it … Does anyone have any Dettol, spirit or cotton?'

'Why?'

'A woman is in the final throes of labour. We are looking for some help in every compartment.'

'Labour pains? In this wilderness?'

'Why? Is there a designated place for labour pains to commence?'

'It is the fault of this system that has rendered us silent and still. God knows how many labour pains are hidden in it. Does anyone ever realize that…'

Finding no help here, the men moved towards the next compartment.

'Huh … these do-gooders!'

A baby cried out from a woman's lap. Children a little older than the baby had forgotten to weep, wail, cry, sob, moan, bawl, whimper, and instead, were clinging to their mothers like scared birds. They were looking at their mothers with questioning eyes, who, in turn, were busy looking around and trying to hear what was being said by the other passengers.

The baby's crying pierced the thoughts, feelings, and chatter.

'Stop him, sister … His throat will be bruised if he goes on like this.'

'Perhaps, he is hungry? Have you given him some water?'

The parents tried everything they could to pacify the child. They showered love and blessings, promises of getting him sweets once they reached home, etc., etc. But that baby refused to be quietened. Several people tried to help; some even held it in their arms and walked up and down to hush it, but to no avail.

'This child is today's man,' the man who had laughed said softly, but everyone heard it and their angry glances fell upon him like daggers.

'Where's the sense in this?'

'Sense? For the train to stop, for our thought processes, for this baby to cry, for you to attempt to pacify the baby … Where is the sense in all this?

'Sense?'

'Brother, if you really can't keep quiet, kindly move to another compartment.'

'Why? Have you inherited this compartment as your personal fiefdom that I should leave it and go away?'

'I have bought a ticket and I know that most people who travel on this line do not buy a ticket but they talk big.'

'This man is getting to be too much … What if he is a foreign agent?'

'He has been trying to spread anxiety for a long time. He has tried to infuse hopelessness amongst us. He opened the door despite all our warnings; it's a different matter that it was…'

'A snake should be crushed before it has splayed its hood…'

'Kill him … Kill him…'

In the commotion, the sound of someone pounding the door loudly was buried. It was only when the armed men of the GRP force emerged from one end of the compartment and gave a few tight slaps to the more rowdy men among the crowd and held the man who was beating the other man that peace was restored. The man's clothes were torn in the melee, blood was coming out from several wounds and gashes, and he was looking absolutely terrified.

'He is causing confusion amongst us…'

'He is trying to infuse hopelessness amongst us…'

'That is not such a grave crime. Why have you taken the law into your own hands?'

'He is surely working for some foreign agency…'

'It looks like you have all lost your mind while sitting here. Whatever you read in the newspapers has made you heap abuses on this poor, unarmed man. Come on … each one of you has to give your name. You have tried to take a man's life.'

'Wah, well said, inspector. If this news were to appear in a newspaper or come out of the mouth of a big man, then it's well and proper. And when we try to … Truly, that's why our country is so backward…'

'Mr Leader, your place is not here in this third-class compartment. You belong on the podium of a council. You are in the wrong place.'

'Leaders don't drop from the skies, dear sir; they arise from third-class compartments, mean streets and dirty drains.'

'Dear Lord, this halted train has caused an entire treatise of law to be printed right here; there is nothing but danger if it remains stationary any longer.'

'Before you go, at least tell us why the train halted. You are an upholder of law. Surely you would have the right information.'

'You should ask the people who have been appointed for this and who draw a salary for doing this job.'

'Sir, at least leave behind a soldier or two here. It is a desolate place … What if some untoward incident were to…'

'It isn't possible to arrange security at every place.'

'You know, even if a robbery takes place here, these people will not come. And you know why? Because they have already performed their duty such as it is!'

'If duty is merely to sniff and go back…'

'This is truly the limit … The train has been halted here for so long. The life and belongings of so many people have been at stake for so long and yet it hasn't made the slightest bit of difference to anyone. There has to be a limit to such lack of feeling!'

'Who is lacking in feeling? Us? All you people? Who is responsible for the train stopping here for so long? The society? The government? After all, we are facing such difficulties because of whom?'

'For now, it is those people who are lacking in feeling who … And the fact is that it too changes its colours according to time and circumstance.'

'We don't know anything…'

'The reason is obvious … the reason…'

'Not reason but reasons … So many that it is difficult for us to decide…'

'It is really quite simple … simple and ordinary…'

'Tell us … tell us … Why didn't you tell us if you knew all along?'

'It is really quite obvious…'

'Then why don't you tell us?'

'Because you won't accept it.'

'Are you a comedian? Or a leader?'

'No, sir, I am neither a comedian nor a leader.'

'Your antics are like…'

'What can I do? I am helpless. Without these antics you wouldn't…'

'Look here, sir, do you intend to tell us or not? Why are you troubling us? Our time…'

'Time? Well said … To appeal to the one thing you don't have, the one thing that was snatched from you a long time ago…'

'Or put another way … Something far heavier than this has been burdened upon us under whose weight we cannot even groan…'

'No, instead the awareness of our precious vote – if indeed it is precious – has been snatched from us and, in our senselessness, we are leading a life that is worse than a corpse's.'

'Brother, this is not the time to display your weighty knowledge, but to find out why the train…'

'Where has that gentleman gone who had said that its reason is…'

'Perhaps to the toilet…'

'It is always so … It has always been so. The person who has the information is always…'

'Brother, I am right here … I had indeed gone to the toilet, although that institution, too, is of no use to us any more. And friends, I am not so knowledgeable either that I will go looking for hideouts. I am…'

'You were saying that…'

'Yes, yes, brother … I am still saying that it is a very simple matter. You and I should go together and find out…'

'Is that all? Is this what you had been going on about for so long?'

'You think this is insignificant?'

'Do you think we hadn't thought of it?'

'If you had thought of it, why have you not done anything about it till now?'

'Leaving behind women, children, the elderly, all our bags and baggage?'

'So, you mean the world held your feet back?'

'The world…?'

'Yes, brother, what else? You believed the words of each and every one of us, and all these things have pushed you into the sea of disbelief and inconstancy.'

'Uff … Brother, we don't have the capacity in our brain to understand these high-sounding words. We are, in any case, at our wits' end with fright and worry; you have simply added to our woes. First you raised our hopes sky high, and when we dug the mountain, what did we get but a…'

'A rat! … We are all rats, my friend, whether you admit it or not. We are the rats who have gone to sleep in the rubble of our mind; we will get up from our sleep only when rat poison is poured down our rat holes. By then, all our exits will be closed…'

'Is any way out open today?'

'Today, we have closed our own paths. Tomorrow, someone else will do it and then no paths will be left open for us … Never ever…'

'Okay, let us say that we get out now … We go ahead and find out why the train has stopped … Then? … What will we do, then?'

'If there is a good enough reason, we will stay quiet; if not, we will complain to the higher-ups.'

'Wah, brother! … Such high-flying talk and then … We will complain! To whom will we complain?'

'What else can you do? These people have a separate department where you can lodge your complaints; we seldom have the guidance or knowledge to avail its service. If an abundance of complaints are lodged there, there's no reason why…'

'Perhaps you don't know, mister, that flies, mosquitoes, dust and cobwebs have taken over the complaint counters, just as offices are run over with cats and dogs. People like you and I don't go there any more.'

'You are speaking metaphorically?'

'No, realistically! Clearly, this shows that you are an intellectual in the true sense of the word.'

'No, brother … Such a big accusation…'

'You talk beautifully … just like an intellectual…'

'You don't know. When we are in a difficult situation and all our paths are blocked then even an ignorant and stupid person can start talking like an intellectual.'

'That is why the production of books is so high in our country. We have a plethora of newspapers and periodicals, an abundance of seminars and lectures … And the result?'

'Exactly what is in front of you … The train has been stopped for a long time and we have descended to talking at an intellectual level.'

'Is there any God's creature who will forsake words and just words, and instead make some arrangements for food and drink?'

'The snack sellers have sold all their wares and are sitting in some corner now playing cards. And water? There isn't water for the toilets, how will there be any water to drink?'

'Everyone will die of hunger and thirst, and their blood will be…'

'It is our neck, so the blood too will be on our neck, won't it?'

'Surely there must be some human habitation nearby. Surely we can find something to eat and drink…'

'Brother, had it been so, by now…'

'That means … that means…'

'It means nothing … Really, it is very simple: we will keep on talking till this train moves again.'

'Even if someone were to die of hunger, thirst, or some other reason?'

'You don't need a reason to die; you just need an excuse.'

'Brother, let us at least decide on one thing: when we reach our destination, we must do something so that an incident such as this is never repeated.'

'Meaning…'

'Really, my dear sir, don't you know we never reach our destination cumulatively? It is always circumstances and situations that…'

'That means we shouldn't do anything? … We should let whatever is happening, happen?'

'If anything is in your control, do it … Bismillah[1] … Who are we to stop you?'

'That means…'

Suddenly, a silence fell; no one had the strength to complete the sentence.

---

1 A verse from the Holy Quran literally meaning 'I begin in the name of Allah…' but often used, as here, to mean 'make a start'.

# THE LAST EXILE

*Syed Muhammad Ashraf*

THE EKKA TURNED a corner on the mud track that ran between the tall kansa bushes, crossed the bridge over the Kali river, and then travelled the remaining four kos so swiftly that the line of pain etched on the forehead of the ekka's solitary traveller – an ascetic-looking old man – became even deeper.

The biggest river of the plains lay ahead – stretching from here to there! The sun had slid down by now and the shadows had lengthened. The river looked frightening at this time.

The old man got off the ekka and shivered. He covered his body with a chadar and then, with brisk steps, began to walk on the narrow path between the temples on the ghats. He walked so far and so swiftly that the evening bells resounding from the temples began to seem like a distant echo. Crossing fields with feet-deep tender wheat, he came to pause beside a small mound. By now, the village was left far behind. In the light of the setting sun, the hibiscus flowers trailing over the little hut changed colours and appeared orange.

The old man approached the small door of the hut, adjusted the ancient manuscript tucked under his arm, and tried to wipe the dust from his feet with a piece of cloth slung over his shoulder, the dirt that had mingled with the evening dew to coat his feet more thickly.

'Baba!' he called out softly. There was fog outside the hut, and darkness inside.

'Come inside.' The two words brought light to the hut that had been as silent and as dark as death until then.

'Let's have some light, Maharaj!' the old man said and wondered: 'What are the emotions visible on my face at this moment? Fear or reverence?'

'Have a light in your heart, my dear,' once again that light-bestowing voice came from inside. He stepped into the darkness inside the hut. By the time the old man's eyes adjusted to the absence of light, the first thing he realized was the thudding of his own heart.

He was sitting at the far end, with his back against the wall.

With quivering steps, the old man moved towards him, and then, fumbling to find his feet, laid his head on them. When the dry skin on his feet was sufficiently drenched in the old man's tears, he put his hand as blessing on the old man's matted locks.

'Light the lamp,' he gestured in one direction. The old man lit a lamp and kept it close beside him. In its light, he saw his face closely for the first time. How peaceful his eyes were in the shade of those long, white eyelashes. The rest of the body didn't seem as though it was attached to those eyes.

'When did you set out from Braj?' the light rose again.

'This morning, before sunrise,' the old man answered softly.

'Have you come to see me for the last time?' the flickering flame of the voice rose and fell.

The old man nodded his head to say yes. Drops of tears fell from his eyes, slid down his white beard and fell into the folds of his warm chadar.

'How did you come to know that it is time for me to go?'

'You had inscribed in the ancient text of our ancestors that when they asked you what gift you would want for your selfless devotion, you remained quiet. They had asked you to take the most precious thing on earth; then, too, you had remained silent. Then they asked if you wanted a long life, to which you had replied, "No, grant me reverence." They had said, "But that is entirely ours." You had replied, 'Life, too, is yours." Then they had said, "Go, our blessings are with you, and the gift of a long life for as long as there is dignity for us on this earth." Or did they say, "Go, dignity is with you for as long as there is life on this earth"? They said this and went away, and you came to live in this hut beside the river where you were born. You tried to hide your secret from the world. A body, similar to yours, was found dead in Benares.'

'How many people know about this?'

'The eldest in the family who inherits the ancient manuscript.'

'Who is that?'

'That is me,' and once again the old man placed his head on his feet. The long eyelashes closed over the eyes and the voice asked softly, 'But you still haven't told me how you came to know that it is time for me to go.'

'All the signs are mentioned in the ancient text,' the old man gestured towards the old manuscript he was carrying with him.

'Do you want something?'

'Yes,' the old man raised his head and said, 'I want to stay with you. The ancient text says that you will be granted the blessed sight of a darshan when the end is upon you. If I am with you, I too will catch a glimpse of that divine sight and I shall be able to partake of the Infinite Joy of Paradise in this very life.'

'What else had I inscribed in the book? It has been almost five hundred years. I have begun to forget now.'

Once again, the old man placed his head on his feet and, with tears streaming down his face, told the name of the river beside which he had prophesied he would breathe his last. Then, that being with the large eyes and a body like a string of bones spoke softly in a tone of utter sadness, 'I have been carrying the gift of a long life and living in this hut for centuries, hiding myself from the world. Do you know the path that goes towards the river?'

'I have made all the preparations to take you to the river. We must leave today.'

'Let us go,' he answered with gravity and steadfastness, and got to his feet. The old man saw that the bones in his ribcage were as clearly visible as the lines in an epic.

By the time they reached the river after journeying for one night and one day, evening had fallen. There was a clamour in the basti at some distance from the river.

'We have come so close to the basti. Shall we go there?' the old man asked him.

'The last moments will be beside the river ... it is written. Why go there?' he answered softly.

'Shall I go by myself?' the old man asked fearfully.

'Go,' he said, looking towards the flowing river.

The old man set off. He returned after some time. 'They are not allowing me to go into the basti.'

'Who is stopping you?'

'The soldiers.'

'Why?'

'They are saying there is a huge crowd inside and that I might get crushed underfoot.'

'Then?'

'They will also not let us remain by the river. Those are their orders.'

'Why is there such a clamour over there?'

The old man saw the soldiers silhouetted in the distance and replied to him in a whisper. He heard and fell silent. The old man saw that the light in his eyes had dimmed somewhat.

'What else is written in the ancient text?'

'You will be so blessed that whoever you wish to see will be able to assume a human form and come here.'

'No, tell me what is written about the day that is to come.'

'Nothing is written on this subject, nothing on what will happen tomorrow.'

'I remember now ... that is where my knowledge had grown weary. I had begun to pant. I had told your ancestor: Whatever I have asked you to write down, consider that enough. I am not God that I know everything.'

'These words of yours are written at the end of the ancient text,' said the old man.

'What is the time of drawing the last breath?' he lifted his lashes.

'It is written in the book that the sun will be in the middle of the sky at that time,' the old man replied.

He closed his eyes.

The old man asked him if he wanted to eat something. When he received a 'no' in response, the old man took his permission, opened the little bundle he was carrying with him, and brought out some food. He had barely finished eating and retied the bundle when the heavy tread of khaki-clad soldiers carrying long weapons in their hands was heard.

'What are you baba type of people doing here? What are you planning?'

The two remained silent.

The soldiers looked suspiciously at the old man's bundle. Then they snatched it and opened it. They were disappointed to find in it a piece of dry roti and a slice of pickle.

He opened his large eyes and looked at the soldiers as he lay on the ground. The soldier who had opened the bundle could not bear the pure lustre of those eyes. He said, 'Baba, we are helpless. We have no power inside the basti. We have been told to guard the boundary. At the moment, there is no one except you here, at the outskirts beside the river. So, naturally we are suspicious and wondering if you are up to no good.'

'Don't worry, my child. We are here to wait for the last moment,' he answered softly.

Then the old man tried to tell something to the soldiers, and to hide something. The soldiers heard and laughed. The old man opened his mouth to say something when he pressed his hand gently from where he lay on the ground and gestured him to stay quiet.

Then the soldiers spoke. 'Look here, babas, there is a great clamour inside the basti. We are barely able to control that. We don't want any further trouble. People in the basti have made all manner of plans to have a darshan in there, and you two are sitting here outside the city limits, beside the river, waiting for your darshan. What a strange thing to say! We, too, have read the ancient texts. You say that he is still alive? Are you making fun of us? Come, move away from the footpath and closer to the river … lest someone fires at you by mistake in the darkness. Understood?'

Suddenly, the loud sound of a whistle was heard. The soldiers left them where they were and ran in the direction of the sound.

'How do you write such fine poetry?' the old man asked.

'Devotion made me write it,' he answered briefly.

After a moment's pause, the old man said, 'How did he describe all the leela so vividly in poetry despite being sightless?'

'An Infinite Love had opened the eyes in his heart. And his devotion was boundless. Whatever this devotion saw, it was poured into poetry. And his language was yours too. You are from Braj. Our words must sound harsh to you?' he asked with a smile.

'No, that isn't so,' the old man said, touching his feet.

'Help me walk till the river.'

When the old man took him close to the river and helped him lie down, a half-bitten moon appeared in the cold sky.

'Tonight is a very difficult night,' he said in a feeble voice.

'And the day that will be tomorrow.' In the pale light of the moon, the old man tried to search for Death on his face.

'Tomorrow will be a difficult day, and a joyous one too.' As his large eyes opened, the old man saw that there was hope in them; some despair too.

'You won't be frightened by their darshan, would you? You won't be scared when you see the spirits in their bodily form?' He closed his eyes as he asked this.

The old man thought for a while and said, 'I am with you, so I will not be scared.' And after a pause, he said, 'It is written in the ancient text that some other spirits too will appear in human form. Do you recognize them all?'

'No, not all. What have we to do with all spirits, my dear? You must pray that when you see them, their faces have the same smile they had when they were granting the boon of a long life and the blessing of dignity and honour.'

'How will I recognize them?' the old man asked.

'You will know. There will be a moon-like halo around their face. Pray, now.'

Suddenly, a loud noise erupted from the basti. The loud clanging of bells could be heard. He lay beside the river, reciting a holy mantra. The old man sat praying beside him. The birds on the trees lining the footpath became agitated and flew across the river.

'Where are the birds going so late in the night?' he asked, stopping his recitation.

The old man broke off his prayer to look towards the sky. 'They are doves. They are leaving the basti to fly away across the river.'

The two of them stayed silent for a long time.

A very loud noise indicated that morning had broken. The same soldiers were running towards them.

'Baba, you have not left yet? At least don't be seen at the outskirts of the basti.'

'There is very little time left. Please, let us stay here,' the old man said in a pleading tone.

'No, you can't, not in full view of everyone! You can enter the river and stand there. You can see everything from there. Your life is in danger here. You should have gone into the basti yesterday.'

The two of them waded into the ice-cold water and stood there, turning their gaze towards the basti's outer limits. The people inside the city were creating a din; all of them were wearing clothes of the same colour, holding long objects in their hands, and speaking aloud in a language he could not understand. He asked the old man, 'What are you thinking, seeing the people of the basti?'

'Nothing. Seeing their clothes, I am reminded of the flowers outside your hut. The flowers had turned such a strange colour at that hour.'

'When the sun is about to set and dusk is settling down, the colours of all the flowers change, my dear,' he spoke softly, in a feeble voice. Suddenly, a trishul rose in the old man's head. The old man looked at the flowing water of the river and asked, 'It was written in the ancient text that the gift of your long life will end when His dignity is demolished. What...'

'What is the time now?' he asked without answering the old man.

'The sun will shortly be in the middle of the sky.' As he spoke these words, the old man's lips began to tremble. A storm erupted somewhere deep within the basti and some strange sounds could be heard.

'What are those sounds?' he asked in a faint voice, stumbling over his words as he stood in the river with his eyes closed.

The old man listened closely and then said, 'It sounds as though brick and rubble are falling.'

'Brick and rubble are falling inside me too, now.' He opened his eyes with great difficulty and gave a clue to what was happening inside him.

'Is it time?' the old man asked in a tone of fear and hope.

He remained silent, though he kept his eyes open.

The river was silent, the sky was silent, and the footpath lying in front of them was silent. All the birds had flown away somewhere from the trees that stood at the basti's edge. The loud sound of falling brick and rubble came from the basti. Startled, the old man tried to see his body that was now submerged in the water up until his neck.

He looked at the old man with a faint but peaceful smile. Suddenly, a loud, anxious rustling could be heard among the bushes lining the basti's boundary. Several people, weeping and wailing, were jumping over the bushes and coming out of the basti. Their faces were either silver or golden.

One of them was wearing a white achkan; in place of his heart was a large, fresh stain of blood.

'Who is that?' he asked in a receding voice.

The old man looked closely and then said that, earlier, in place of that bloodstain there used to be something else, something he couldn't remember now.

A rustling was heard among the bushes again. This time, an old, half-dressed man emerged, holding something in his hand.

With great difficulty, he opened his eyes and asked, 'Is that a dead snake in his hand?'

The old man saw the stooping, bent man come out of the basti and run far away.

'No, whatever he is holding in his hand is moving. It could be a live snake, or perhaps it is a walking stick. He used to walk with a stick, always.'

For the last time, a loud sound was heard among the bushes lining the basti's outskirts, as though those who were inside were desperately trying to come out. Three people emerged: two handsome young men and a beautiful woman. They were rushing out of the basti in a mad frenzy.

The old man looked at him. He was looking at the three people with his eyes wide open. Suddenly, a silence descended upon the universe. The river stopped its flow for a moment, and he let his body sink into the waters with reverence, fear, despair and peace.

The old man came out of the river in order to see the three people more closely.

The clothes on the bodies of the handsome young men and the beautiful woman were torn to shreds. The wounds from bricks and stones had scarred their arms. The crowns on their heads had slipped around their eyes, and all three had halos like the moon around their head. The old man bent his head and offered them salutation with folded hands, tore every single page from the ancient book of history, and then, falling down on the ground beside the river, covered his face and entire body with dirt.

# A NIGHT'S PARADISE

*Faiyaz Riffat*

THERE WERE THREE of them; all three had sworn to be together for the rest of their lives and to die together. Who were they, where had they come from, what was their religion, which part of India did they come from – these were questions they had never asked each other. The one thing they had in common was – unemployment … relentless unemployment, which had brought them inextricably close to each other.

Their past clung to their forehead like grains of sand. Their present was cloaked in thick layers of mist. They lived solely on the sweet dreams of a glorious future.

And now…

Now one of them was dead.

His corpse lay squarely in the middle of the footpath where, just seconds ago, his companions had covered it with a ragged old sheet. The sheet, being a bit short, couldn't cover the dead man's body fully, leaving his face exposed. Anyone looking at that face could tell that the man had died at the pinnacle of youth. He had barely begun to grow his whiskers.

Now his face wore a deathly pallor. His hollow cheekbones stood out on his gaunt face. Yet the beauty of that youthful face clearly shone through, even in death. That classically handsome long face, aquiline nose and limpid blue eyes could soften the most stony-hearted of men.

The young man had died of abject poverty. Death had not been due to natural causes. The distressing severity of his circumstances and ceaseless financial hardships had nudged him into the arms of death much, much before his time. Weakened by hunger and starvation, he had been swept away like a twig in a gust of wind. And with him were gone his dreams and aspirations, lost forever in some surging unknown ocean.

He had come to the city with such dreams, but now those dreams lay trampled in the dust. The dazzling city lights, the buildings that reached up to the sky, the array of beautiful faces – all remained strangers to him.

No one befriended him. No one ever extended a friendly hand towards him. He kept knocking at the doors of those buildings that rose to the skies, but no one ever answered his knocks. He trudged along on the brightly lit streets until every bone in his body ached and his shoes wore off.

But no one ever asked him to pause awhile, to rest his weary limbs. There was not a single sheltering tree on those brightly lit, endless city streets where he could find rest and respite. His eyes ricocheted off countless beautifully groomed faces, but no one ever brought their face close to his.

The beautiful faces took in his dishevelled clothes in one quick glance and blithely went their own heedless way.

People were gathering donations for the dead man's last rites. His two companions stood silently, with bowed heads, on either end of his dead body. Their mouths had run dry and their tongues had grown tired of extolling their late friend's virtues.

Until last night, the dead man had been sitting with them at a roadside shack, laughing and joking over a pao roll and a small cup of tea. Afterwards, they had gone to their usual places on the footpath. When they woke up in the morning, they found him dead. They wept and wailed.

Witnessing their loud lamentations, a crowd slowly gathered and started dropping big and small coins for the dead man's last rites, each according to his own status, on the grimy sheet. Some people who were more God-fearing than others, left one-, two-, even five-rupee notes to secure a place for themselves in heaven.

In this manner, two hundred and thirty-four rupees and five paisa were collected.

The dead man's two friends looked meaningfully into each other's eyes. Casting a quick, all-seeing glance in every direction, one said, 'Everything is okay. Two hundred and thirty-four rupees and five paisa is quite enough. It won't be wise to delay any further. It's dark already. The last rites should be finished.' A muffled giggle escaped him by the time he uttered the last sentence. He looked at the dead man and spoke admiringly, 'What a wonderful scheme my friend has concocted! Imagine earning two hundred and thirty-four rupees and five paisa in a single day!' He tugged at the sheet covering the dead man and said, 'Get up quickly now. First, we'll go and have a grand meal somewhere, then we'll go to a brothel, maybe even get drunk.'

The dead man continued to lie there – mute and still as a corpse. The dead man's friend shook him and said again, 'Great acting, man! Now get up quickly or someone might call the police and we'll be in real trouble.'

The dead man heard the word 'police' and immediately came to life.

He uncoiled like a spring, and in the blink of an eye, all three disappeared down a dark alley. They were heading for a certain place on Byculla Road where, on the fifth floor of the seventh building, Punjabi, Sindhi, Gujarati, Bhutani, Santhali, Rajasthani, Marathi, Anglo-Indian and Burmese girls practised the age-old profession. One, two, or more – there were enough here to last all night long. You could take your pick from among the young and the old, the novices and experienced hands. Country-made 'Horse brand' liquor was also available. You could order mashed potatoes, fruit chaat, mince samosas and tandoori roti. For two hundred and thirty-four rupees and five paisa you could buy all this for one night.

As they approached the building, they looked around with sharp, penetrating eyes. Then they sprinted up to the fifth floor. A decrepit old madam measured the three young men with her world-weary eyes.

In a flash, a bevy of brightly coloured fairies surrounded them. Each of the three men picked the girl of his choice by looping an arm around her waist. They picked up a bottle of booze each, ordered their food, and placed the grubby notes and rust-speckled coins on the madam's wizened old palms.

Then they sat down and began to talk. Their beloveds for the night sat beside them and kept plying them with drinks. When their intoxication had soared up their spinal cords and exploded in the back of their skull, they began to hurl the choicest abuses at each other. Swaying in the arms of their beloveds for the night, they tottered off to their rooms.

All night long, they partook the pleasures of paradise they had bought for one night.

By the time morning dawned, there was bedlam in the entire building.

The madam woke up, hearing the girls squawking and crying. She found the three young men sleeping peacefully. When she tried to wake them, their necks lolled over and blue flecks of foam frothed from their mouth.

According to the forensic report, the cause of death was spurious liquor.

# A LETTER OF CONDOLENCE FOR THE LIVING

*Khalid Jawed*

> 'We wanted to create a snake. Perhaps it was a dot that wanted to become a snake but midway it changed its mind and changed its direction. Now it has become something else: hanging midway in its incompleteness, wavering here and there in the air.'
>
> – Klaishmey

NEARLY LOSING HIS senses because of a pain in his abdomen that was growing steadily like a storm gathering momentum, at first he ran along one side of the road. Then, without giving a thought to the dangerous traffic, he crossed the road and ran on the other side. He ran for a long distance on that side too. Here, too, there was a glimmering bazaar, clean, well-lit shops, and beautiful, glistening houses. Almost all the houses were the same, made according to city guidelines, looking like a row of identical graves. Each grave was a copy of the other, rather every death a duplicate of the other.

Disappointed, he slumped against an electric pole and began to pant.

He thought he should get off the main road and head into the narrow alleys that were cutting each other at a ninety-degree angle. He might find it there. He quickly got off the highway and entered a narrow street. There was a big park up ahead. The streets, too, were glimmering like the main road. Electric bulbs were lit. There wasn't a trace of darkness in any corner. And there he was – desperately seeking darkness. If only there was at least a wall. If only there was the dark shadow of some house.

Like a thief, he began to circle the front and back of the houses. But not a single house provided a shade. The houses had nothing but a front-facing facade. And a bright, clean one at that!

The entire city was gleaming and clean like a white, starched kurta-pyjama that had freshly been brought from a laundry. He sniffed. The air was redolent with the strong fragrance of good-quality detergent used to wash clothes.

If only a gust of foul smell would come from somewhere. But just then, the scent of flowering plants wafted in from the park. The floral scent mingled with the pleasant smell of the washing powder. He became more worried than ever.

He should go into the alley facing him, he thought, and in an almost comic haste, like an agitated toad, he entered the alley with a hop and a skip and a jump. But here, too, was an identical park and the same fragrance, and the same sort of people sitting huddled together, whispering, smiling and laughing among themselves.

Where are the drains? He looked around in search of an open drain, but all the drains were possibly underground.

Animals? Where are the animals?

But all the animals had possibly been slaughtered due to hygienic reasons.

And not just pigs, even cats and dogs.

Unfortunately, he had not seen any dogs or heard them barking.

Disappointed, he sat down with a thud. However, he felt as though he was not sitting on the ground but on a white sheet spread out on it – a sheet that was floating in air. Perhaps he had felt dizzy as he had sat down. So he got to his feet at once and spread both his hands wide to save himself from the next dizzy spell. The pain was increasing. So were the dizzy spells. Moving his arms rapidly, he tried his best to keep the dizziness at bay. Then he moved, tottering on his feet and swaying a little as he entered the narrow alley to his left, but again, this alley too met up with the wide, brightly lit main road from whence he had come.

Once again, he ran through the dangerous traffic and made his way across the main road to the other side. Walking slowly on the footpath, he began to move southwards. Beside the road were balloon sellers and carts selling chat. Lush, ripe women were eating golgappas, their lipstick-painted mouths opened wide in an obscene fashion.

He stopped and looked at the sky, his mouth open in an obscene manner like those of the women. The sky was turning red and black. His mouth was filled with the December fog, and his nose began to run. One after the other, he sneezed several times and nearly yelped with pain. He felt as though a ruthless dagger had been thrust into his penis with the force of his sneezing and his entire body shook in agony.

Was there no ditch, no pond, no pool?

Was there no gutter, no drain?

But no, the world didn't have any such places any more.

Any rubbish heap anywhere?

No, all the rubbish heaps had been transformed into flower-filled gardens.

His glance fell on a glimmering signboard which had a red-coloured hangman's noose and the following inscription:

> The penalty for those found smoking on the road is a sentence of death. Anyone found guilty of polluting the environment will be hanged in full public view.

He was terror-stricken. A chill came over him. His old leather jacket had big gaping holes. The cold and the fog entered through these holes and crouched near his chest under the grubby blue shirt that had not been washed for an age. This blue shirt too had holes. The fog began to dampen the hair on his chest. The cold air entered his battered old shoes and coiled around his feet. He cast another glance towards the sky. For a second he saw the moon, but then, in the blink of an eye, it instantly went behind the canopy of the fog.

He got off the footpath and began to walk on the black, coal-tarred road.

The pain was increasing like the hand of a bad clock – fitfully, jerkily, sporadically.

The night had deepened. The market began to close down. The bustle on the road was winding down but the number of policemen on the road began to increase. To ensure that the cleanliness was maintained, policemen in white uniforms were stationed at close intervals. Their uniforms were fragrant with the scent of detergent and flowers. And they were so white that the black, coal-tarred road appeared unimaginably white in the glare of their whiteness. They were fully prepared to hang, right here in full public view on the road, anyone who was smoking a cigarette or beedi, or spreading any manner of pollutant in the air. They carried a noose fashioned from smooth white rope in their hands. They were self-sufficient hangmen in their own right, competent to execute orders. At that moment, he felt as though his belly would rip open. Like a madman, he ran into the alley on his right, as though he was being chased by the Angel of Death.

In front of him he saw a house where light was spilling out from the windows. In that light he looked closely at his clumsy, swaying shadow, and then, not thinking any further, he began to pound loudly at the door of the house. The door was not locked from inside. It opened at the pounding of his hands.

Inside, two men and two women were sitting at a dining table.

He stood before them and folded his hands.

'I have to urinate … that's all … Believe me, that's all … For God's sake, just to urinate…' he pleaded. No one even got up from the table.

The two men were twins, and so were the women. There wasn't any difference in their ages either. An ill-omened and hard-to-comprehend uniformity hung over the dining table.

They were all intent upon drinking their soup.

'I have come to your house because I need to urinate. I understand that that is wrong and entirely uncouth behaviour. After all, your house is not a public urinal where any Tom, Dick and Harry can barge in. But take me for a poor, uninvited guest, and please forgive me. I am in great pain. My bladder is bursting. I have a stone in my kidney. For pity's sake, show me the way to the bathroom! I shall be grateful to you for the rest of my life. I shall be in your debt forever.'

Tears began to fall from his eyes. He clutched his abdomen with both his hands. Such was his agony that he nearly doubled up with pain. But thinking this to be bad manners, he immediately removed his hands from his abdomen and once again folded them as he stood before them.

The man looked at his twin and the woman looked at hers. Then all four of them began to look at the white ceiling.

'I am helpless, very helpless, and also very sick. Have pity on me, please!' he begged, shivering under the combined effects of the cold and the pain. His trembling was like a dog's that had caught a chill and was now in the grip of a fever.

'We are going to hand you over to the police. Tell us: where have you come from?' The four of them spoke in unison. The male and female voices combined to turn this sentence into a frightening noise.

'No … For God's sake, no…' Scared by the frightful sound of the four voices that spoke in a chorus, he pleaded. 'Believe me, please, I am not a thief. I am a decent man. I too must be living somewhere in this world, but I have got lost today. I have forgotten the way to my home. This city seems like a stranger to me. Perhaps I have been asleep for a very long time or been unconscious. Or it could be that both my mind and memory have been damaged. But this I can say with absolute certainty, and you must believe me, that I have come into your house only to urinate, and for no other reason. Outside on the street, on the crossroad and the alleys, I could not see any public urinal anywhere. I looked everywhere. I have been knocking about all evening. I have been wandering around in alleys and lanes, but the punishment for urinating on the streets is death by hanging. Like hunting dogs, they are all in search of me, holding the white noose of the gallows.'

Saying this he sat down on his knees in front of them, keeping his hands folded all the while, and began to shiver like a scared, wet, miserable kitten. The mingled scent of soap and flowers emanated from their clothes. Sometimes, this scent would be overpowered by the smell of roasted cabbage.

One of the men picked up a glistening white dinner knife, got off the chair, and came towards him.

'You miserable thief, don't you know there are no toilets in homes?' he growled.

'What do you mean?' This time, his eyes opened wide not with pain but with surprise.

'Come on, phone the police,' one man said to the other.

The second man said to the first woman, 'Come on, phone the police.'

The first woman said to the second woman, 'Come on, phone the police.'

He had always found twins to be scary and ominous. Their power, hatred and oppression increased manifold. They seemed against the order of a well-disposed universe. If a person is throwing you to the ground to slaughter you, at least you can beg for mercy from his other companions, or at the very least make entreaties with your eyes. But if perchance all those companions are lookalikes or twins, then this is simply not possible.

'No, sorry, forgive me! I don't wish to be killed at their hands! I don't want to die! I am not a thief…' and he kept sitting on his knees in front of them with his hands folded in entreaty.

Time and time again these words escaped his lips in a trembling voice.

'Urine … only urine … I am innocent … I am ill…'

'You are mad! Diseases and filth spread if you do such things in your home. No one does such repulsive and disgusting things now. Come on, get out. Go to a hospital and get your head examined.'

Again, the four of them spoke in unison.

But he couldn't understand a word in the din of this speech. He just sat there in front of them, bleating.

Then the man who was holding the glistening dinner knife in his hand came closer. He felt the white handle of the gleaming knife land on his head.

He rolled over backwards towards the door, without volition, like an empty tin.

He was thrown out of the house like a lowly insect.

With a loud sound, the door was bolted from inside.

Lying flat on his face on the ground, he felt an empty copper bowl lying beside his head and heard the frightening 'drip-drip' of a dreadful drop of blood that was intermittently dropping into the bowl.

After a long time, he was able to get up by resting both his hands on the ground. He felt as though the pain had gone from his abdomen. The urge to pass urine too had gone. But his head was aching most terribly, and stars were dancing before his eyes. Wrapped in a sheet of fog, swaying on his feet, having no idea in which direction he was heading, he began to move forward. The noise of traffic was lessening on the roads. Silence was deepening but the cold was intensifying. The chill had its own noise. His skin, not his ears, could hear the sounds in the same way as a snake hears sounds. His heart and his lungs were shrinking, terrified by the frightening black noise of the cold.

Once again, he could feel the pain in his abdomen and the full disclosure of the fact that the pain that lived in his belly had, in an attempt to pacify his aching head, crawled out of his abdomen and penis and come up to his head for a few moments and was now going back to its rightful place.

He felt an intense compulsion to urinate. He could not control himself. Without any further thought and without worrying about his life, he began to undo the buttons of his fly with trembling fingers. He was absolutely ready to urinate on this desolate street.

He forgot about the nooses that were patrolling every few steps, as though they were not made of rope but dust and dirt and that he had seen them some time in his dream.

But the moment he opened the buttons of his fly, he felt as though there was a piece of ice lodged there. The urge to urinate had turned into the burning fire of ice. Numbed in this hell of ice, his fingers felt as though they were being slashed when they came in contact with this cold, deep wound made by the ice. The icy cold winds of the December night and the swirling ribbons of mist began to enter the open fly.

It was possible that, at a subconscious level, he was unable to urinate because he was scared, he thought. And once again he remembered the hangmen, dressed in white uniforms, smelling of flowers and soap, marching in the streets, holding a noose.

Their very thought frightened him, and he forgot to button up his fly.

Terribly overwrought and confused, he began to quickly walk towards the path that led to the main street. Suddenly, he stopped at one place. It was a cinema hall. Suddenly, he was filled with happiness and hope. Surely there would be a urinal here. He remembered the row of urinal booths in Jagat Talkies.

There was still time before the night show got over. He saw the gatekeepers of the cinema hall preparing to open up the locks from behind the doors.

He leapt towards the cinema hall's security guard. Here, too, there was the scent of flowers and soap.

The security guard looked closely at him.

'Open the gate for a minute, brother,' he pleaded.

'What have you come to do here now? The film is nearly over. Had you come an hour earlier, I would have quietly seated you in the balcony and charged you only ten rupees. Nothing can be done now. The heroine has given up her life by now. The film is over.'

'I haven't come to see the film. I have to urinate.'

'Are you mad?'

'No, brother; I have a stone in my kidney. My belly is bursting. I feel I might die. Please let me go to one of the urinals inside the hall. I will pee and come back,' he pleaded even more piteously.

'Go, away! Urinals are not made here any more ... Go away! Or else, I will call the police,' the guard shouted at him, waving his stick in the air.

He raised his eyes and saw a gigantic poster fluttering above the cinema hall. The swaying poster looked like a noose.

Like a frightened animal, he scooted off from there in a mad sprint. Running like that caused a sharp, shooting pain in his lower abdomen, as though a pointed pebble had lodged itself there. This horrifying pain sometimes travelled down to his penis and sometimes moved towards his navel. In that state of acute pain and discomfort, he ran for a long while. No one knows whether anyone in that city could hear the sound of his running steps or not, but he certainly heard the whistle of a train from somewhere far away as he ran.

He stopped and tried to control his breathing.

He decided to go to the railway station. There would certainly be urinals there. After all, passengers come from far and wide. He tried to reassure himself as he was reminded of his childhood where it would be written in big bold letters at the railway stations:

'Public Latrine – Gents' and 'Public Latrine – Ladies'

Once again, the whistle of a train sounded somewhere nearby, and guessing its direction from the sound, he got off the main road and began to move towards the right side.

As it turned out, he was not wrong. He found himself standing in front of a small but gleaming railway station. There were no crowds. Only one or two travellers could be seen. The station was amazingly clean. The building was white and seemed to be drenched in the sweet fragrance of attar. He came running into the station as though his train was about to leave. The platform was deserted like a white strip under which iron railings ran far into the distance and a network of red and green signals glimmered at its far end.

He ran from one end of the platform to the other. At several places he bumped into hawkers who hurled curses at him. But he couldn't see what he was searching for.

Helpless and exhausted, he looked towards an elderly passenger. He had an oddly shaped bag slung from his shoulder that looked like a large football and had ears like a donkey's on top of it. He was looking at the iron tracks unblinkingly.

'Sir,' he asked, 'where is the toilet?'

'What?' A sound like a siren escaped from the old man's lips.

'Toilet … I mean the place where you go to relieve yourself.'

The old man looked at him closely, as did he at the old man.

A deep gash divided the old man's face into two parts. It seemed as though it was not one but two faces that were staring at him. There was a long wound from the forehead to the chin: a long pink-and-white streak.

'I have to urinate. My penis is swelling up. I have a stone in my kidney. I will die if I don't pass urine. For pity's sake, tell me where I can go to relieve myself,' he parroted these oft-repeated sentences.

'Where have you come from?' His voice indeed sounded like a siren.

'Sir, believe me, at this moment I can't remember. The intensity of my pain has dulled my brain. My heart is sinking,' he answered in a quivering voice.

'Have you forgotten that there are no urinals anywhere in the world any longer?'

'Surely you are joking. I am in agony.'

'Do I look like the sort of person who will joke? Humour doesn't figure in my scheme of things. Can't you see I am a serious person? I am a professor.' The siren sounded very loudly.

'Oh, sorry! How could I have known? I just wanted to know where to urinate…'

'Are you blind? Can't you see the mark of knowledge and learning on my face? Every true professor has this scar on their face.'

He heard several sirens signifying danger. At that very moment, a train came speeding down, making a terrifyingly loud noise and shaking the tracks. It didn't stop at this station. After the train had passed, he felt an immense silence, as though he were standing in the midst of deep, dense jungle.

'See, you stupid man, there's a police post outside the station. If you make any mention of your disgusting and repulsive desire, you will be hanged to death immediately. No suit is filed against someone guilty of polluting the environment. He's simply hanged right away.'

A frightening sermon was emanating from between the sirens that escaped through the old man's breaths. God knows why the pointed pebble pricking the inside of his penis had dislodged itself and moved hither and thither. The pain seemed almost tolerable for a while.

'Sir, do the people of this city no longer answer the call of nature and relieve themselves?' he asked somewhat timidly.

'Yes. Although I know you are either mad or a spy, I will still answer your question. Ever since the university has retired me, people have stopped asking me questions. When a professor is not asked a question for a very long time, the scar of knowledge and learning on his face begins to itch, and itching is, in itself, a sign of filth.'

The old man paused for a while and then began to speak as though he were addressing a huge gathering.

'It has been an age, it has been an age since human beings walked about carrying a bundle of filth with them. The fact that man had a body was, in itself, the biggest sin. The customs and practices of the body tie the spirit in knots. The root of all evil was man's body. Listen carefully! Why are you repeatedly clutching your stomach? It is nothing save a deception, a delusion, a chimera, a mirage! This addiction of the body had been afflicting humans since the beginning of Creation, and that is why they were thrown down from the heavens, and that is why deliverance of the soul became steadily difficult.'

He decided that the old man was mad, and so he got off the platform and sat down cross-legged on the white, blemish-free tracks. Sitting in that pose made his abdomen feel even more taut and stretched. His trousers began to pull uncomfortably against his waist. He could feel his breath constricting in his chest. He immediately got back on his feet.

The old man was very tall. In comparison, he felt like a dwarf. He lifted his face and helplessly began to listen to the old man's lecture in the hope that, once he had got everything off his chest, he might tell him some way in which he could relieve himself.

'Listen … listen carefully,' the siren thundered.

'Man's body is a bundle of filth, and filth is the treasure trove of desires. In the name of love and romance, the body has always drawn a curtain over its filthy needs. But because it is not yet possible to free oneself of the essence, the people who are in charge of city-planning have – with the help of the collaboration between science, religion and philosophy – done away with "love" and driven it out of the city limits. And, therefore, this and other such attempts have totally purified the body of its excesses. All the animals have been sent down to the netherworld. This new scientific society is entirely vegetarian. The new generation has to go looking for the meaning of the word "meat" in battered, old dictionaries.'

'Please do me the kindness of showing me the way to the nearest hospital. I am ill. At least there I will be able to rid myself of this wretched urine that is filled inside me,' ignoring the old man's words completely, he entreated restlessly.

'You are not ill, your soul is sick. If you interrupt me again, you will face dire consequences.' The old man glared at him in a frightening manner. The long, deep gash on his face began to glimmer like the skin of a poisonous snake.

More than half the night had passed. Suddenly, gusts of cold wind began to blow over the platform. The iron tracks and the red and green signals were shrouded in mist.

The hair on his head began to feel damp. As he stood there with his face upturned, he began to feel dizzy again. His tired feet had swollen most unbearably beneath his torn, old shoes. Since he hadn't passed urine for such a long time, there was a swelling in his entire body. He felt a piercing ache in his kidneys.

In a bid to control his pain, every now and then he would bite his dry, parched lower lip with his teeth.

'People now go to the hospital only to cure their souls. The body has rid itself of phlegm, cough, pus and germs. The hospitals have all been turned into lunatic asylums.'

For a moment, he felt like beating the old man – who had been making a fool of him for so long and annoying him so terribly – and turning him into mincemeat, but at that point he didn't have the strength to even lift his hand. Gathering all his courage, he could only say sarcastically: 'Sir, do people no longer die now?'

'No, they don't; death is a thing of the past. Only he who has become filthy or will spread filth will die. Death must be lying somewhere on the rubbish heap of history; now, there aren't even any rats left in the world to nibble away at it.'

The professor's tone had become conspiratorial. He had brought his voice almost to the pitch of a whisper when he suddenly boomed loudly: 'Now, this pure and clean city is in the shadow of a great thrall. As soon as it has gained control over bodily frailties and its related abominations and impurities, death has scurried away with its tail between its legs. Ha! Ha!'

The old man opened his mouth wide and let out a terrifying guffaw. Several thousand petrifying shrill sirens echoed simultaneously. And the ears of the donkey, that was made on the bag that hung from his shoulder, began to bob up and down.

'So children are not born now?' Horrified, he groaned.

'Of course they are born; it's just that they don't die. They will have a longer lifespan. They will become old but still they will never die ... Like me! I shall live forever!'

'How are children born without any filth?'

'Children are no longer born from their mother's wombs. Instead, they are born in a clean, beautiful, flower-filled garden. There is no need for a woman's filthy body for them; it is sufficient to have the desire to have a child in your mind and spirit. The new world is entirely and totally a man's world. We have turned all of women's destructive secrets into mere shadows. They have been freed of the soiled rags filled with the dirty blood of their monthly cycles. A woman was the first proposer of sin. Now, no decent and respectable woman can commit the sin of love. Everything has been rendered clean and pure.'

'Look here, professor, enough is enough! You have made fun of a poor, ill person to your heart's content, but now, for God's sake, just tell me where I can go to pass urine?'

Since he could think of nothing else, he bent down before the old man and began to plead and beg with folded hands – hands that were trembling with cold and pain.

The wound on the professor's face began to wriggle and writhe once again, like a snake.

Because of that long, deep gash – that divided his face into two equal halves – the old professor looked like a devil or an evil spirit.

'The bodies of humans only appear like bodies on the surface. After all, who doesn't know that what you see is not real or true? The bodies have turned entirely into minds. Is this not the highest stage of evolution? The bodies have been rid of all manner of filth and muck, and rendered pure. The human body is a true and faithful reflection of the soul,' the devil divulged further, making a sound like a whistle or a siren.

'But I want to pass—' he could not complete the sentence because the professor interrupted him.

'Look here, if you are really a spy of the government, by now you would know that I am strongly in favour of this community development project wherein city-planning boards, in collaboration with the department of health, have launched a movement to clean up the entire world. All the intellectuals from the fields of science, philosophy and religion are a part of this great project. And if you are not a spy, then you really must go to the hospital, where only mental diseases are treated and not pain in any part of the body. Pain is only a delusion. The mind is beyond any sort of pain. You are not a body; you are a soul, just a soul.'

The old professor was showing no signs of letting up. The platform seemed more desolate than ever. From all around, the merciless and relentless fragrance of detergent and flowers wafted in.

For a moment, he felt as though he had indeed gone mad. He felt an uncontrollable urge to smell the unmistakable stench of urine. Summoning all the strength of his entire body to his throat, he said, 'You son of a pig! You despicable devil! I am about to pee in your mouth!'

Saying this, he leapt towards the old man like a wild beast, but almost instantly stumbled and stepped back. He felt as though the long gash on the old man's face had sprung at him like a snake.

Suddenly, a whistle sounded, and he could see them coming towards him. Holding the hangman's noose in their hands, those men in white uniforms were coming closer.

But he didn't want to die. He didn't want to hang from a scaffold beside a highway.[1]

---

1 This is an extract comprising the first section; the long short story has two more, though somewhat shorter, sections.

# SUFFOCATION

*Khurshid Akram*

IT WAS A scorching hot day. A lot of passengers were waiting restlessly for the bus to arrive at the bus stop. Because the bus hadn't come for a very long time, the number of passengers was increasing. Seeing that the bus was late and the swelling crowd waiting for it, the faces of those who had already been waiting at the bus stop for a long time began to look more anxious and strained. Those who were only just joining the crowd were worried to see the large crowd already assembled; how would they get into the bus?

The crowd was a motley one. There were those with bright faces, who were dressed in nice clothes. There were village folk with loosely tied headscarves, dressed in crumpled dirty clothes, a simple wooden staff in their hand and a bundle over their shoulders. There was no shortage of women in that crowd either. Well-dressed, well made-up ones, as well as others in soiled clothes and with dry, wilted faces. Women of different ages, complexions and body types, as well as children of different ages and heights – all were standing, waiting at the bus stop. Everyone was mopping the sweat from their face, neck and brow. They would lift their hands to shield their eyes as they looked in the direction from which the bus was expected to come; disappointed, they would again wipe the sweat that was trickling down their face, forehead and neck, and lick their dry lips with their parched tongue in a vain attempt to moisten them. Some people wore goggles; they too were looking in the direction from which the bus was expected but without shielding their eyes with their hands. Sometimes, they would take off the goggles to wipe the sweat from their eyes. They would look around with naked eyes. When the harsh sunlight and the hot, sand-laden air hit their eyes, they felt as though blisters were forming on their eyes and would immediately put their goggles back on. And they would wonder: How are all these people standing here with their eyes unshielded against the harsh glare of the sun? But it was not possible to think any more at that time, and they would once again crane their heads to look in the direction from which the bus was expected to arrive.

In the far distance, a bus turned a corner and appeared on the straight road leading to the bus stop. All those who had been craning their heads to sight the bus saw it trundling towards them trailing a cloud of dust. A sense of relief was immediately visible on their faces. But once they looked at the people standing or sitting around them, they became a little worried. There were so many passengers, and only one bus! But at least the bus was coming! That was something! A strange sense of relief mingled with a strange sort of anxiety was visible on the faces of the passengers. Everyone was trying to prepare themselves, in whatever way they could, to be the first to get into the bus as soon as it stopped and grab a seat. After standing for so long in the scorching sun, all of them wanted only one thing: to manage to secure a seat in the bus.

The bus reached the stop but had not even halted fully when the more able-bodied, agile and clever among the passengers leapt towards the doors. In the rush to get inside, a melee broke out. The gate was tiny, barely wide enough to allow one or, at best, two people to pass through. At a time, four or five persons were trying to squeeze through it to gain entry. In that jostling, no one could get on the bus. Everyone was exerting every ounce of their strength to emerge victorious in that scuffle to somehow board the bus and secure a seat. If one or two from that crowd managed to shove and elbow their way in, the remaining got in position to successfully squeeze through. The others who were standing around would gather their courage to join the crowd in the hope of travelling in some degree of comfort if they too were to secure a seat, but seeing the jostling at the gate and finding themselves unable to match the pushing and shoving, they would fall back. Having given up hope of securing a seat, now their only wish was to somehow board the bus and manage to find a place to stand which was, ideally, near a window, where they would not get pushed and shoved too much. If one stands at the back, the chances of getting pushed are greater. There is a risk in standing in the front too. If the bus were to collide with another bus or lorry coming from the front, the greater number of fatalities is among the passengers in the front. And these drivers drive so rashly, as though human life is of no value. So what if they do not value their own life, at least they should spare a thought for the lives of those who are travelling in their vehicle? But who can say anything to them? If you request them to show some caution, they call you a coward and make fun of you. And so, taking everything into consideration, it is best to stand in the middle of the bus; this is, relatively, the safest place.

All the seats were occupied. Passengers of different age, height, colour and status had succeeded in finding a seat for themselves. The great majority were those who looked fitter and stronger than the others, though some weak-looking people were also seen occupying these seats, making one wonder how they had survived the pushing and jostling at the gate. It was possible that some of them had jumped in through the windows. One could see a certain satisfaction on the faces of those who were occupying the seats for, clearly, they would now pass the journey seated in comfort. By now, most people were entering the bus with relative ease. It was almost entirely full, both in the front and back. The driver had parked the bus at the bus stop and gone to a nearby dhaba for a pouch of country liquor.

Soon, the bus was entirely full, but there were still people left on the pavement who were waiting to board the bus at any cost. In the eyes of the weak and the timid among them, there was a wild hope: if only they could get into the bus somehow or the other! And in their heart was a hopelessness: for surely there was no way that they could get into that already overcrowded bus, and, if perchance they could somehow manage to board it, how would they ever manage to survive the long journey? And yet, everyone *had* to get into that bus. The bus would move, the driver would brake hard, and automatically some space would be created after every jolt, they told themselves. But those who had already boarded the bus tried to stop the newcomers from entering.

'Brother, why are you getting in? You can see there is no space,' said one man who had only very recently managed to get in himself. The ones below were insistent upon getting in, come what may. Their bodies were bathed in sweat. The women were the worst affected in that crush. Sometimes, they would turn around and glare at the men who were taking advantage of the terrible crowd and leaning against them. Some were cursing the bus, the heat, the driver, the conductor and the crowd – all at one go! Small children were clamouring: 'It's so hot!' 'It's so hot!' 'Water!' 'Water!' The conductor was rudely and brusquely asking the passengers inside the bus to make space for those still waiting outside, and also chivvying the ones still waiting to board to somehow get in.

'Hunhh! It benefits him to have more people crammed into the bus. So what if people are stuffed like potatoes in a sack…' said a passenger who was standing on one foot. Several people standing near him looked at him as though they agreed with him. The conductor pretended not to have heard him at all and said, 'It's completely empty inside. Come! The brothers who are inside should move a bit further … there is so much space. Come on, come on, move a little!'

The passengers in the middle of the bus stood their ground; they knew that if they moved an inch there would be a stampede here too, as there had been near the doors. But those passengers who had already boarded got pushed to the middle by the jostling and shoving of those who were still trying to get in. Distress inside, perspiration outside – this was the sum total of their being. As though completely oblivious to all this, those who were seated were gazing serenely out of the windows; even though the view outside was the same as it was a while ago. Every once in a while, some among the seated passengers would cast a restless glance at the passengers who were standing. A feeling of kindness would surge inside them, but they would swiftly turn their gaze away, telling themselves, what could they possibly do? Even if they were to give their seat to any one person, it would not solve the situation for all the rest. And then, how would they themselves endure the journey in this dire situation?

By now the bus was literally packed to the brim. A great many passengers were standing on one foot. They couldn't find the space to set down the second foot. And if they were to put their foot down on someone else's, that person would cry out angrily: 'Can't you see? You are stepping on my foot!'

'It can't be helped. Can't you see? I don't have the space to put even one foot down properly. I am literally standing on my toes. If it wasn't for the rod up here, I would have … But if you were to shift your foot slightly, I would be able to…'

'Where do I shift it to? There isn't any place. I myself have been standing on one foot. I haven't been able to set down my other foot.'

It wasn't as though there was no space between the two feet. There was, but not enough for a third foot to be planted.

One of the standing passengers addressed the passenger seated facing him, 'Brother, if you were to shift just a little, one person can sit next to you.' Both the seated passengers looked strangely at the man who was standing. If anything, they settled down more comfortably on their seats. And, once again, they turned their gaze and began to look out of the window.

By now, there wasn't even space to put down the proverbial seed of sesame inside the bus. Yet, people were still trying to climb aboard. The rancid smell of sweat permeated the entire bus. It was almost as though a puff of vapour was emanating from every body.

'Come on, brother, start the bus. How many more people are you going to stuff in?'

'Can't you see the state of people in here? You are only concerned with your profit. Call the driver! Start the bus!'

'They are selfish! Tagore had said: Had man not been selfish, this world would have been paradise.' A passenger tried to convey the essence of the entire scenario in that statement, but his words went over the heads of most of the passengers. From somewhere, a hushed voice spoke in a mocking tone, 'Q... ui ... et!' And the passenger who had spoken earlier fell silent.

The conductor looked at the crowd, moved towards the driver's seat and switched on the radio; then he went off to call the driver. A song was playing on the radio: '*Zindagi ik safar hai suhana...*' ('Life is a pleasant journey...') The words were constantly being repeated. Perhaps the record had got stuck. A few people, annoyed by the sweltering heat and the loud, persistent music, looked for the conductor, hoping to ask him to turn the radio off. Others were unthinkingly repeating the words of the song. Still others, who were standing on both feet, stood their ground more securely. Those who were standing on one foot were constantly searching for the tiniest space so that they could put their other foot down. Those who had managed to reach the footboard were now anxious to board the bus at any cost. Those who were still standing on the road were engaged in the struggle to somehow set foot on the footboard.

Seeing the driver coming towards them with the conductor, the passengers were relieved; when the bus moved, there would be some air. There would be some respite. The driver was twirling his moustaches and strolling as though he didn't have a care in the world. Swaying carelessly, he sat down in his seat. Now, another song was playing on the radio: '*Kya hua tera vaada, vo qasam vo iraada…*' ('What happened to your promise, your vows, your will…')

The conductor came and sat down on the seat reserved for him and blew his whistle.

'Come on, brothers, hurry up and get your tickets!'

With a slight jerk, the bus started. The passengers breathed a sigh of relief. After travelling for a short while, the driver applied the brakes suddenly; all the passengers in the bus were jolted. Even those with their feet planted firmly on the floor felt uprooted. Those with their feet mid-air now found space to plant their dangling feet. The ones who were seated sat down more firmly after a slight jerk, as comfortable as ever. The standing passengers fell or leaned hard against each other. Collecting themselves, they began admonishing the people standing behind them in annoyed tones to stand up straight. The jolts had created some space in the bus. Now almost all the standing passengers stood with comparatively less discomfort.

The bus was travelling at great speed on the highway. The conductor was issuing the tickets. The driver, with his hands on the steering wheel and his eyes on the road, was singing along with the song playing on the radio, his body swaying to the beat. The bus was racing on. Puffs of hot air and dust were coming into the bus. The air was scalding the body, but at least the sweat was drying off. The stink, however, was spreading. After a while, the heat of the sun lessened, and with it the temperature went down a little.

Soon, some clouds could be spotted in the sky. The air no longer felt hot. Puffs of cloud were scudding across the sky and the air now began to feel pleasing, even delightful. After every few intervals, the conductor would call out from his seat: 'Whoever has not bought a ticket yet should buy it. At the check post coming up, if the inspector catches you without a ticket, you will be fined.'

The sound of fat drops of rain falling on the metal roof could be heard. The bus was speeding through the rain and the raindrops kept coming down thicker and faster. Everyone in the bus let out a sigh of relief. The air was definitely pleasant now. The rain was coming down hard. The passengers seated beside the windows pulled down the glass panes.

Fields spread out far into the distance on either side of the road. The tall and majestic trees, dotted about the landscape, were swaying like drunks. Lush green sheaves of tender wheat danced in the rain. The steady trickle of rain was washing their face clean, making their colour glow even brighter. The breeze, too, was playing with the leaves and the wheat stalks, fondling and teasing them. The scene outside was truly bewitching. The song on the radio had changed to: '*Hum laaye hain toofan se kashti nikaal ke / Iss desh to rakhna mere bachchon sambhal ke…*' ('We have steered this boat through the storm / Keep this country safe, my children…').

A woman was nursing her baby, her breast bare. Another child, whose face and hands were grubby, was clinging to her legs half asleep. Perhaps the child had grown weary crying and become drowsy. The tears had left some dried, barren lines on its cheeks, like the grass that dries up and withers when a snake slithers past.

The bus was speeding along and almost all the passengers were gazing out at the verdant green fields on either side with some satisfaction. The ones who were standing were still leaning, to some extent or the other, on those nearest them. But no one was angrily admonishing them to stand straight. At best, they squirmed a little. And then let their body loose. The rain was coming down in torrents. After some time, it was no longer pleasant inside the bus as it had been a while ago. All the windowpanes being down, no air could come in or go out. Soon, people began to feel uncomfortable. It became still and claustrophobic inside, and soon, the suffocation intensified. One man, who was not especially old but was perhaps suffering from some respiratory disease, began to look more restless than the others. He began to pant. Soon, others too began to feel anxious; they were finding it difficult to breathe. All the doors and windows remained shut because the rain had not let up.

Finally, a young man, who was standing next to the man who was finding it difficult to breathe, addressed the passenger seated next to the window: 'Sir, please open the window for a little while.'

While he spoke with seeming meekness, the anger boiling inside him was evident in his tone. The passenger seated next to the window glared at him. 'Can't you see? It is raining!' Then, with a show of great surprise, he raised his shoulders and said, 'Hunh! All sorts of idiots get into the bus.'

'Don't you have any manners? Is this any way to speak? What a selfish person you are! Can't you see that a person standing next to you is finding it difficult to breathe?' the young man burst out.

'Look here, boy, control your tongue! What can I do if he's finding it hard to breathe? Hard to breathe…' and he raised his voice and began to laugh. 'Brother, why do something that you find hard to do?'

Quite thoughtlessly, everyone around laughed out loud at this statement. This angered the young man even further.

'Come on, be sensible. Open the window. Someone is finding it hard to breathe and you are only thinking of not getting wet!'

'If someone is finding it hard to breathe, they should get off and breathe in the fresh air. Brother conductor, stop the bus and let this gentleman get off so he can breathe.' The seated passenger spoke with sarcasm dripping from his voice.

By now, many of the other passengers too were finding the suffocation unbearable. They began to agree with the young man. Buoyed by this support, the young man said, 'Look here, open the window a little,' and he stretched his hand to pull up the windowpane. But the man seated next to the window raised his hand swiftly and knocked the young man's hand away.

'Yes! Yes! Raise the windowpane and let in some fresh air!' Many voices spoke in unison as several people, by now fed up of the suffocation inside the bus, came out in open support of the young man.

The man with the respiratory problem began to pant for breath. The young man's anger increased even more. By now he was ready to fight with the seated passenger in order to open the window by a show of brute force if necessary.

The man who was seated behind spoke in support of the man beside the window: 'What is this high-handed bullying? You are forcibly opening someone's window ... Won't he get wet?'

And then, several passengers seated far and near them began to speak up, voicing their support in different ways.

The standing passengers were dropping with exhaustion and almost breathless with suffocation. And so, they put up a united front and unanimously supported the young man's bid to open the window. Encouraged by this show of solidarity, the young man got into a scuffle with the passenger seated beside the window. The seated passenger was equally adamant to not allow the window to be opened. Soon, a full-fledged fight broke out between the two. In a bid to show his camaraderie, the passenger seated behind shoved the young man. It enraged the young man even further. All the passengers who were standing tut-tutted their displeasure, but no one was willing to act on behalf of the young man. Seeing him at a disadvantage, the man with the respiratory disease came to his rescue, despite his difficulty in breathing. He pulled the young man aside to remove him from the scuffle. The young man was somewhat deflated by now. All the standing passengers were looking at him with sympathy and helplessness. Anger blazed on their faces at the unfairness that had been meted out to him. Yet no one was ready to back him up in that skirmish.

'If you don't want to get wet, you can stand in my place. I will get wet, but I will keep the window open so that at least some air can come in,' another standing passenger spoke up with great aplomb, addressing the passenger seated near the window.

'Okay, so I am willing to admit that you must be the cleverest man on the planet. You want to grab my seat on the pretext of letting in some air.' Hearing this sarcastic response, several other seated passengers laughed out loud.

'Hey, conductor, open the window! It's becoming difficult to breathe!' another standing passenger called out.

'Brothers, why are you fighting? What is all this noise about? Whoever has not bought a ticket yet, please buy one. If the inspector at the check post finds anyone travelling without a ticket, there will be a fine.' The conductor did his duty and went back to gazing out of the window.

Peace reigned inside the bus for a short while. The bus kept moving. The rain kept falling. The suffocation kept increasing. Several people began to pant as they took in short, shallow breaths. Some of the seated passengers began to doze off, or tried to do so. Those who were awake were so intent on gazing at the scene outside that they were not so affected by the suffocation. Those who were standing searched for resources deep inside themselves to cope with the suffocation.

A song was playing on the radio: '*Chalo dildaar chalo chaand ke paar chalo, hum hain tayyar, chalo...*' ('Come, my dearest, let us go across the moon, I am ready, let us go...')

Sometimes, the driver would let go off the wheel and clap with both his hands as he repeated the words of the song playing on the radio. The conductor kept clacking his ticket-issuing device to keep tempo.

After some time, a robust-looking passenger took out a cigarette from his pocket and lit it. Gradually, smoke from the smouldering cigarette began to waft around.

'What a strange fellow this is! It's already so suffocating inside, and he is smoking a cigarette!'

'Listen! When I find it hard to breathe, I always smoke a cigarette.'

'But it is prohibited to smoke inside a bus,' said a man who looked sensible.

'Where does it say it is prohibited?' asked the smoker indolently.

'There!' the sensible-looking man pointed. But the 'No' had been scratched out; now, only 'Smoking' was written. The man fumed with a helpless rage but stayed silent. The smoker took a long drag on his cigarette and quite deliberately blew the smoke in that man's face. Soon after, another passenger too lit a cigarette. Then, one after another, several passengers began to light cigarettes in an attempt to gain control over their breathing, and took long, deep draws on them. It was already very closed and suffocating. The smoke from the cigarettes made it worse. The passengers began to draw quick, shallow breaths. Those who were puffing away at their cigarettes looked content. Everybody in the bus was experiencing some degree of difficulty in breathing, even those who were seated and seemingly engrossed in enjoying the scenery outside.

One of the seated passengers looked at those who were standing. He, too, was finding it difficult to breathe. Without caring about the rain, he opened the window near him.

A gust of cool, fresh breeze wafted in, singing and swaying. The faces of the passengers perked up. Drops of rain too came in. The man seated next to the passenger who had opened the window looked at him with murderous eyes and quickly closed the window.

Across the glass window, fields stretched until the far distance. Tender green sheaves of wheat, bent under the weight of their grains, danced in the rain. The scene outside was very romantic; inside, it was difficult to breathe. Every now and then there would be the sound of someone coughing, clearing their throat, or wheezing. Every face bore signs of restlessness, suffocation, anger and helplessness. Exhausted, helpless passengers stood with mute tongues. Lit cigarettes emitted puffs of smoke. And the bus raced on at full speed.

# LIFE IS NOT A STORY

*Salam Bin Razzaq*

JAMILA THOUGHT LONG and hard over her decision: was she about to commit a mistake – a mistake that would never be corrected? At the same time, she felt she had no other option. If she were to weaken the slightest bit today, she would spend the rest of her life feeling choked and regretful. This was the only way to rid herself of the suffocation that was deepening all around her like a dense, all-enveloping fog, though there were also many doubts and dilemmas on this path, much fear of disgrace and dishonour, as well as the anger and wrath of near and dear ones. The community would raise fingers; she might be alienated from her younger brothers and sisters. Yet this path tugged at her heartstrings as though she had spotted a dense shade-giving tree on a blisteringly hot day.

In a delightful flight of fancy, her heart began to beat swiftly, and a strangely sweet tremor rippled through her body. Overwhelmed by her own feelings, she closed her eyes. The moment she did so, Aslam came and stood before her – smiling, moving his hands over his shiny, black hair, calling out to her with his arms wide open! Uff, what a delightful vision it was! Blood raced through her veins at the thought that, in a few short hours, this imagined sight would turn into reality! But in the very next moment, a dreadful shadow stood between her and the vision. It was none other than her father, Maulvi Jamaluddin, who was glaring at her with wrathful eyes. He held a rosary of fat beads in his hands. He was quickly running the beads through his fingers and mumbling something under his breath. Aslam took one look at him, and his outstretched arms fell to his sides. In the blink of an eye, Aslam's figure disappeared from sight.

She felt as though Maulvi Jamaluddin was saying to her, 'What are you contemplating? The entire world looks at your father for guidance, and you, despite being the daughter of Maulvi Jamaluddin, are setting off on a path that is the path of the misguided? The path of those who will soon be visited by God's wrath?'

Anxiously, she opened her eyes. The whimpering, sighing light of the night bulb was spread in the room, and on either side, her three sisters – Akthari, Akbari and Anwari – were fast asleep, their arms looped around each other's necks. Her younger brother, Rasheed, was sleeping outside in the veranda. Her mother lay huddled in a corner, looking like a little bundle of rags. Despite having a pillow, her right hand was curled near her head. She always slept like this, as though she was about to set off on a long journey. One couldn't quite call it sleeping though; it was more like a momentary rest and respite, as though in a matter of a few moments she had to get up and set off on another journey. Her newborn sister, Sajida, was suckling as she lay next to her mother. God alone knows if there was any milk in the mother's wizened breasts or whether the infant was suckling at those dried-up breasts only out of sheer habit. Young Shakil lay beside Sajida; he was smiling faintly in his sleep. The space on the mother's other side was meant for their father, Maulvi Jamaluddin, but he was not there. He had left on Allah's path three days ago.

He used to be a machine operator in a factory, once upon a time. He earned a decent wage. He had a two-room house in a chawl. Everything was going well when, suddenly, there was a strike at the factory. The strike went on for so long that eventually the factory was locked down. Nearly four hundred to four hundred and fifty workers were laid off. Jamaluddin was one of them. In those long days of unemployment, he began to offer the namaz. As he began to pray regularly, a noticeable change came over him. He grew a beard. He stopped wearing pants and shirts; instead, he started dressing in a kurta-pyjama with a topi. Offering the namaz five times a day and travelling with the jamaat[1] to offer daawat soon

1 Referring to the Tablighi Jamaat (literally meaning 'Society of Preachers'), a body that works with Muslims giving them the daawat or 'invitation' to be better Muslims, to pray regularly and observe the Five Pillars of Islam more rigorously. Members of the jamaat travel in groups and are recognizable from their appearance: they sport beards with moustaches, are clad in kurta-pyjama and topi, with the pyjama well above their ankles; they are usually carrying their meagre belongings rolled up in their bedding on their shoulders. The Tablighi

became his routine. During this time, he learned a great many verses from the Holy Quran and could recite them from memory. In his tours with the jamaat, his knowledge of religious matters increased considerably.

One day, the Bengali maulvi who used to teach the neighbourhood children in the madrasa nearby, died. The mohalla committee decided to appoint Jamaluddin as the teacher in the madrasa. And so, Shaikh Jamaluddin became Maulvi Jamaluddin. He began to receive a salary of three thousand rupees from the mohalla committee. Each month, he would place the entire amount in his wife's hands, and for the rest of the month remain blissfully unconcerned about all the financial matters pertaining to his family's budget and expenses. Even if the wife tried to draw his attention towards the less-than-happy circumstances in their home, there would not be the slightest lessening in the majesty and glory of his contentment. On the one hand, the financial situation became dire year after year, and on the other, every two or three years a new guest would arrive. When the fourth child arrived, the wife tried to caution him as gently as she could. Indirectly, she also stressed, 'Jamila is growing up; we should now think about her.'

---

Jamaat encourages its followers to undertake short-term preaching missions (khuruj), lasting from a few days to a few months, in groups of usually forty days to four months, to preach to fellow Muslims, reminding them of the core teachings of the Prophet Muhammad and encouraging them to attend mosque prayers and sermons. Members travel, eat, sleep, wash and pray together in the mosques, and often observe strict regimens relating to dress and personal grooming.

Maulvi Jamaluddin was a quintessentially religious person. Offering the namaz five times a day and chiding those who didn't pray was the sole purpose of his life. From head to toe, he had devoted himself entirely to religion. There was such a large dent on his forehead – from the many prostrations he offered daily – that it was the first thing that caught one's attention if one looked at him; it was enough to overwhelm the viewer with piety. He was not a maulvi by virtue of any theological training or study; he simply began to be addressed as 'Maulvi Sahab' by everyone because he taught the Holy Quran to the children from the neighbourhood.

Maulvi Sahab thundered at his wife, 'What is this nonsense? Have you people lost all faith in Allah? Who are we to worry about anyone? It is written very clearly in the Quran: "*Wallahu Khairur Raziqeen*".[2] He who gives birth feeds too. He who provides food to a peacock or a locust, do you think He is not concerned about you and me? Remember, children are a sign of God's bounty and generosity, and to turn one's face away from His Mercy is the worst form of ingratitude for His gifts of munificence.'

Maulvi Sahab paused to draw breath, looked hither and thither, and in a slightly lowered voice, said, 'Listen, a husband is a woman's God in the here and now. Disobeying your God in this world is tantamount to disobeying your Allah.'

The poor wife's feeble protest snapped in the face of his mighty arguments, like the last breaths of an ailing patient. And so, despite the wife's protests and protestations, a fifth child came into the world, weeping and wailing.

---

2 From Surah al-Jumah (62:1), it means 'And Allah is the Best of Providers'.

It was about this time that Jamila came of age. She was studying in the eighth standard those days. One day, when she noticed blood-red spots on her salwar, she panicked and ran, huffing and panting all the way home. Flinging her school satchel aside, she hid her head in her mother's lap and burst out crying. Seeing her in tears, the mother too was very alarmed. But when she asked Jamila repeatedly and she told her – amidst many hiccups – that blood was coming out from the place she passed urine, and that now she was no longer fit to show her face to anyone, the mother clutched her to her bosom and exclaimed, 'Arre, you scared me out of my wits! You silly girl! It just means you have grown up. Come, get up, wash your face, drink some cold milk … everything will be all right.'

That night, as Maulvi Sahab was eating his dinner, the mother seized an opportunity, and waving her handheld fan, spoke in a hushed tone, 'Listen … Jamila has grown up … She used the cloth for the first time today.'[3]

Maulvi Sahab continued to eat but glared at her and said, 'So soon?'

'It's hardly early. Next month she will complete thirteen and step into her fourteenth year.'

'All right, then. Make her stay at home now. She has studied as much as she needed to,' he spoke in a dry tone.

---

3 The Urdu original uses the expression '*kapda liya hai*', referring to the practice of mothers teaching girls to use old rags and fashion them into makeshift 'pads' which would be secured in place with drawstrings looped around the waist. The practice still continues in many areas where sanitary napkins are either not available or not affordable.

Jamila's mother had thought he would be happy to hear this news. But far from being pleased, when he issued his Talibani edict, she was enraged. She answered sharply, 'What are you saying? She is so fond of studying. She comes first in class every year. Everybody praises her, and you … you are shutting the gates of learning on her! I will not listen to you on this. I will educate her for as long as she wishes to study.'

Seeing his wife in a temper, Maulvi Sahab became a bit nervous. His arched brows lowered somewhat. However, holding on to his male ego and his machismo, he said, 'All right, all right. But first arrange for a burqa for her. I lower my head with shame when I see her walking up and down the street with her head uncovered.'

The mother bought a new burqa for Jamila, and Jamila began to wear it. Initially, she found it difficult to walk in a burqa; on several occasions, she tripped and fell. She tried to complain to her mother, but the mother made the position amply clear: 'No, no, if you don't wear the burqa, your Abbu will put an end to your schooling.'

Willy-nilly, Jamila had to learn to tolerate the burqa. And with time, that all-enveloping garment became a part of her very being.

Jamila passed the matric exam with a first class. The school committee offered her a scholarship to study in college, but Maulvi Sahab flatly refused to allow her to go to college. Some members of the school committee tried to persuade him, but to no avail.

For as long as Jamila went to school, she was not especially concerned about her home. She did know that her mother scrimped and saved to somehow meet the household expenses. But she had never had to bother herself too much, because the mother did all the worrying. Seeing her mother, she would be reminded of the iron rod affixed at the top of tall buildings, the rod that takes upon itself all the might of the thunder and lightning, keeping safe the building beneath it. But when she finished school and began to sit at home, all those niggling little worries began to stick to her like leeches. Seeing the precarious condition of the family and the mother's failing health, she was seriously perturbed. And now, when her mother was pregnant for the sixth time, Jamila cursed her father in her heart.

Without letting anyone know, Jamila managed to do a nursery teachers' training course from a private institution. Soon this would come in very handy. A new school opened in the neighbourhood. Their neighbour, Aaso Khala's husband, served as a member of the school committee. Upon his recommendation, Jamila got a job as a primary school teacher there. When Jamila placed her first salary of four thousand five hundred rupees in her mother's hands, the mother's fingers trembled with a strange, unknown happiness. She embraced Jamila, and uncontrollable tears began to course down her cheeks. Once again, Maulvi Sahab was opposed to the idea of Jamila going out to work, but the mother tried her best to reason with him: 'Four thousand five hundred rupees will be coming in the house. What is wrong with that? It will lessen your burden a little. And it isn't as though she has to travel miles and miles; she only has to go a few steps down the road in this very neighbourhood.'

Jamila had been working for two years now. Maulvi Sahab had nearly stopped coming home. He was always unconcerned about the family and household; now he engrossed himself in matters of daawat with greater nonchalance and freedom from all familial responsibilities. He would spend the entire day in the madarsa and the mosque. He would narrate the Hadith and explain matters pertaining to faith to those who came to offer namaz. Once in a while, he would go home, that too to claim his conjugal rights, for most of his nights were spent at the mosque. Now, the responsibility of running the house fell on Jamila, for the mother had become so frail that she would begin to pant even while speaking. Even in this condition, a child had been born to her a year and a half ago. At the urging of their neighbour, Aaso Khala, an operation was performed immediately after the seventh child had been delivered. Initially, the mother hid this from Maulvi Sahab, but soon he came to know. He was very angry and didn't come home for many days. He stopped talking, but the mother was past caring. At least she had been saved from the nightly pawing and pouncing; at least that was some saving grace. But for how long? One night, Maulvi Sahab got into her quilt saying, 'Don't you know, to kill one's spirit is asceticism, and asceticism is forbidden in Islam?'

Jamila could see that there was nothing left in her mother. Underneath the loose, ill-fitting clothes, dry, cracked skin stretched over a handful of bones. Her eyes were sunken, her cheeks hollowed. Her mother was completely wrung out, and yet her father was continuing to wring her. She used to wonder if he wouldn't stop till there was a drop of life left in her. Sometimes she wanted to tell her father exactly what she thought of him without any consideration for his age, and the cloak of piety that he went about wearing would be torn to shreds. But she could do no more than swallow her anger. When her thoughts began to stifle her, she would close her eyes and lose herself in thoughts of Aslam. The mere thought of Aslam was like a magical box in which her many colourful dreams were safely shut.

Aslam was a scouts' teacher in the school she worked in. Tall, not too fair, with ordinary features, but always with a heart-tugging smile on his lips; talking to him brought a strange sort of tranquillity to her. On the last Parents' Day, Jamila had prepared a chorus with the little girls in her charge. When the children, dressed in white frocks and pink scarves appeared on a darkened stage singing '*Lab pe aati hai dua ban ke tamanna meri...*'[4] holding lit candles, suddenly the stage was flooded with light when they came to the lines: '*Duur duniya ka mire dum se andhera ho jaaye / Har jagah mere chamkane se ujala ho jaaye*'. The audience loved this sight so much that for a long time the hall kept resounding with applause. The headmistress had fulsome praise for Jamila, as did the other staff members. The next day, she was seated in

4 Refers to the poem entitled '*Bachche ki Dua*' ('A Child's Prayer') by the Urdu poet Sir Muhammad Iqbal whose opening lines are:

*Lab pe aati hai dua ban ke tamanna meri*
*Zindagi shama ki surat ho Khudaya meri!*
*Duur duniya ka mire dam se andhera ho jaye!*
*Har jagah mere chamakne se ujala ho jaye!*

My wish rises to my lips like a prayer
O Lord, make my life like that of a candle
So I may remove darkness from the world
So I may spread light with my brightness

the staff room in her 'off period' preparing a chart when Aslam entered. He congratulated her on the successful chorus song of the previous day's programme: 'Your chorus was the life and soul of the function!'

Jamila thanked him with a shy smile and bent her head, seeming engrossed in her work though her attention was fully on Aslam. He was wiping the perspiration on his forehead with a handkerchief. For a few minutes, there was utter silence in the room. Then, Aslam's voice rose: 'Jamila Sahiba! I want to say something to you!' Startled, Jamila raised her head. Her heart thudded. Aslam was standing facing the calendar hanging on the wall. Without turning around, he said, 'If I had a mother or a sister, I would have asked them to speak on my behalf...'

He paused for a moment, then continued, 'Would you agree to be my partner in life?' A certain constancy was brimming in his smiling eyes. At that moment, Jamila was overwhelmed with a surge of love for him. She wanted to get up and plant a wordless kiss on his cheek. But she couldn't do anything of the sort. She sat there, silently, with her heart thudding and her head lowered. After a short pause, Aslam spoke again. 'I am waiting to hear your answer.'

Jamila slowly raised her lowered lashes. Aslam was looking at her, every pore of his body, from head to toe, waiting for her answer. All she could say was, 'Why don't you come to our house, please...' and she immediately lowered her eyes.

'I have heard your father is very stern.'

'My mother is very nice,' Jamila blurted out and instantly hid her face in both her hands.

Seeing this gesture, something akin to lightning coursed through Aslam's entire body. Every pore in his body bloomed with happiness, but all he said was, 'Thank you!' And then, swaying like a drunk, he left the staff room. And so, in a matter of a few moments, all those stages of the journey of love were crossed which, sometimes, take years and years of hard work. Aslam came to their home on Eid on the pretext of offering Eid greetings. Jamila had already told her mother about him, albeit indirectly. One look at Aslam and the mother was completely besotted, but Maulvi Sahab became evasive. Perhaps it was no longer easy to let go of the four thousand five hundred rupees every month.

A few days later, when Aslam tried to get an inkling of her father's views about him, Jamila lowered her head. Her eyes filled with tears. By now, Aslam had begun to understand Jamila's words of silence, and these, after all, were tears that had emerged from the deepest recesses of her being. Gently, he held her hand and, raising her chin with one finger, he peered into her eyes and spoke lovingly, 'Jami! You are a brave girl! Don't shed tears and become weak. I am with you…'

The words 'I am with you…' were spoken with a blink of his eyes accompanied with a smile, and with such utter confidence that all the disquiet in Jamila's heart was purged and, impulsively, she flung her arms around Aslam, smiling in the midst of her tears.

Ah, there was such contentment in his arms! With her head resting on his broad chest, Jamila felt that the world was a ball that she could kick away any moment. Aslam was whispering in her ear, 'Don't worry. I have an uncle who lives in Pune. We shall wait for another month or so, but if the ice in your father's brain doesn't melt by then, I shall land up at your house with my uncle and ask for your hand in marriage…'

'What if he still doesn't agree?'

'What then…? Then I too shall behave with him in the same manner that Prithviraj Chauhan did with Jai Chand.'[5]

Aslam spoke the last line with all the flourish of a film hero, and Jamila burst out laughing despite her tears.

'You will wait for me at the door with a varmala, won't you?'

'Do you even need to ask that, my prince?' Jamila said and put her head back on Aslam's chest.

Barely a week had passed when Maulvi Sahab announced that he was leaving for a Tablighi tour for four months, that he would return after completing three chilla.[6]

'But what will happen to me and the children in these four months?' the mother protested.

Maulvi Sahab produced his counter argument: 'You are so concerned with worldly matters that you have no care or concern for the Day of Judgement, the day on which all your good and bad deeds will be taken into account. One has to make some sacrifices if one is working for one's faith. The people from the madrasa will come and give you some money every month; and then there is Jamila bitiya too. Allah looks out for those who worry about their faith.'

When Jamila conveyed this news to Aslam, at first, he was at a loss for words. He was also very angry with Maulvi Sahab, but,

---

5 The reference is to the mythical love story of King Prithviraj Chauhan who eloped with Samyogita, the daughter of Jai Chand, the king of Kannauj.

6 Chilla refers to the forty-month period of retreat when a person withdraws from the daily world, spending all his time in prayer and meditation. People often go in groups, mostly males, spending their days in a mosque, living simply.

mindful of Jamila's feelings, he swallowed his anger and, with a wan smile, managed to say, 'Now I shall have to enact the character of Prithviraj Chauhan.'

In a sorrowful tone, Jamila said, 'How can you joke about this, Aslam? I haven't been able to sleep all night.'

Holding both her hands in his own, he spoke lovingly, 'I am not joking, Jami! We have only one path for us – the path of Prithviraj Chauhan!'

'I don't know why you are obsessed with Prithviraj Chauhan,' Jamila said with a grimace.

'Look here, Jami … I think your father has gone so far ahead on the road of religion that he has forgotten the way home. And so, we have to forge our own path.'

Jamila didn't say anything. She just looked questioningly at Aslam.

'I have a suggestion. You won't get unduly alarmed, will you?' Aslam asked.

'You are with me, aren't you…?'

'You trust me, don't you?'

'More than I trust myself.'

'Then listen … We should leave for Pune tomorrow itself by the Asiad bus.[7] I will inform my uncle. He will make all the arrangements. We will have a nikah when we reach there.'

'What are you saying?' A slight scream of surprise and fear escaped Jamila's lips.

---

7 The Maharashtra State Road Transport Corporation (MSRTC) Mumbai–Pune bus stand is popularly called the Asiad stand and the buses that ply on this route called the Asiad buses.

'What I am saying is absolutely correct; we have no other way.'

'Ammi will never be able to accept it,' Jamila said in a trembling voice.

'Hear me out; we will perform our nikah and return by the evening. For now, there is no need to tell Ammi anything. Tell her gradually, after taking her into confidence. In any case, she is not against our marriage.'

'No, Aslam! I am finding all this very strange!'

'Look, Jami, this is our only way out. You know your father will never give us his permission to get married. But once he knows that our nikah has been solemnized, he will have no other option but to accept its validity. You are legally an adult.' Aslam stopped for a moment and looked carefully at Jamila. Then he continued, 'I can understand your dilemma, Jami. You are worried about your mother and siblings, aren't you? And rightly so! But remember, all the responsibilities that are just yours today will be yours and mine tomorrow after we are married.'

'Aslam…!' Jamila's lips moved as though she wanted to say something, but surprise and happiness choked her voice. She looked at Aslam. Tears of gratitude filled her eyes. Aslam cupped her face in both his hands and gently kissed her forehead.

They decided to meet the next morning at seven at the Asiad bus stand. She told her mother that she would be going on a picnic with some girlfriends and would return by the evening. The mother happily granted her permission.

All night, Jamila tossed and turned on her bed. If perchance she slept for a while, then some frightening dream would jolt her awake. She dreamt that she was walking in a dark tunnel forever and ever, and the tunnel was showing no signs of coming to an end. Ya Allah! Is there any way out of this endless tunnel? Suddenly, she would spot someone walking ahead of her, holding a flaming torch aloft. Even in the pitch darkness, she recognized him. It could be none other than Aslam. She called out to him – 'Aslam! Aslam!' Aslam turned around, but what was this? It wasn't Aslam. Her feet were rooted to the ground in terror because it was her father, Maulvi Jamaluddin, looking at her with eyes emitting bright-hot embers.

Sometimes she thought: If this marriage was a like a normal wedding, how much fun and excitement there would be! The house would be filled with guests. The rituals of haldi, ubtan and mehndi would be under way. Songs would be sung to the beat of the drum. People would be up all night. The house would be redolent with the scent of attar and flowers. Her sisters would be chirping about gaily and her mother would be bursting with happiness. And Abbu … The thought of her father made her tremble. He was thundering, 'Stop all this nonsense…'

All night long, she drifted in and out of sleep and wakefulness.

'*Allah hu Akbar! Allah hu Akbar*!' The sound of the azan wafted up to her ears and she got up in a flurry.

Surely this was the call to the fajr prayer. She got to her feet, washed her face, performed the wuzu, rolled out her prayer mat and stood on her feet to offer the namaz. Her brothers, sisters and mother were all sleeping, heedless.

As always, she raised her hands in supplication after the prayer. She began to pray: '*Rabb-e ighfarwa-arhamwa an-ta khairulraahe min*'[8] – O my dear Lord! Forgive us our sins and show us Your mercy for You are the Most Merciful.

Suddenly, her body was engulfed with tremors as she prayed and tears began to stream from her eyes. A whirlwind rose in her chest, and it seemed as though a wounded bird was trapped and fluttering in her throat. She was almost crying with loud hiccups when she thrust her dupatta in her mouth with all her strength. Some of her hiccups were smothered, but she was panting with the strength of her emotions. Swiftly, she went to the clay pitcher and drank a full glass of water. Gradually, her breathing became normal. She heard her mother's sleepy voice call out, 'Jamila, shall I make tea? Have a cup of tea at least before you go!'

Quickly she answered, 'No, Ma, I will have it in the canteen. I am getting late; you rest…'

'Go carefully, my child…'

'Don't worry, Ma, Allah Haf—'

Jamila put on her burqa, slung her shoulder bag, and went out. She found an autorickshaw a few steps away. As she sat in it, she glanced at her wristwatch. It was a quarter to seven. The bus would leave at 7.15. It would take her fifteen to twenty minutes to reach the bus stop. Normally, she turned back the face-covering of her burqa after leaving home, but today, to be safe, she kept it in place. She spotted Aslam as soon as the autorickshaw entered the bus depot. He was waiting for her with a bag slung from his shoulder and a newspaper in his hand. She paid the driver and climbed out of the autorickshaw. Now she flicked back the niqab covering her

8 Meaning, 'My Lord, forgive and have mercy, and You are the best of the merciful.' (Quran 23:118).

face. Aslam leapt towards her and said, 'Jami! Have you seen the newspaper today?'

He looked a bit apprehensive.

'No … Why?'

'Come with me,' he said and headed towards the canteen. Jamila flicked the niqab back to cover her face and began walking with him. Seeing Aslam looking worried, she too became anxious. A thousand nervous anxieties began to bubble up inside her. They reached the canteen and chose a corner table. When both were seated, Aslam looked about in all directions, then spoke softly to her, 'Jami, it seems we will have to postpone our plans.'

'Why?' Jamila's anxiety was turning into fear.

'Maulvi Sahab and his associates have been arrested at the border.'

'Ya Allah!' Jamila felt as though she had been struck by lightning.

'Be brave,' Aslam said, putting his hand over hers.

'Who told you?' Jamila's voice was quivering beneath the burqa.

'It's printed in the newspaper … He was travelling with his jamaat near the border when he was arrested by security forces under suspicion of crossing the border. He has been taken to a nearby police post for questioning.'

Jamila began to cry.

'Jami, control yourself! He is not alone; the entire jamaat is with him. He has merely been arrested under suspicion … In a day or two, we will get the news that he has been released.'

Jamila didn't say anything. But behind the burqa, her body was trembling; every now and then, a hiccup or two escaped her lips.

'Jami, if you lose heart like this, what will happen to your family? Come, I will find you an autorickshaw; go home. I will come over and see you in an hour or so. Meanwhile, I will also speak to Ansari Sahab, the chairman of the school committee. We will find a way. This isn't a problem of Maulvi Sahab alone; it concerns the entire jamaat. Here ... drink some tea. Then, we will go.'

Dear readers, having come thus far, the short-story writer wanted to end the story on a hopeful note: namely, that Jamila comes home and, as Aslam has promised her, the two will get married when the situation improves. After all, Jamila has complete faith in Aslam. She believes he will fulfil his promise to her.

But, dear readers, Life is not a story! A fiction writer has the right to end his story wherever he wishes or turn it in any direction he chooses. But no one has control over the swift and strong currents of Life – not even the writer! Sometimes, the current of Life is so strong that the writer's pen is swept away like a twig. Something like that happened here too.

After keeping him in custody for a month and a half, the police released Maulvi Jamaluddin because they could not find any proof against him. Upon his release, he returned home like a lost, pillaged wayfarer – down at heel, broken in spirit, shattered by the humiliation and dishonour of his arrest. He came home and fell so ill that, within fifteen days, he passed away. The shock caused a paralytic stroke in Jamila's mother, and she became bedridden. Her younger brother, Rasheed, failed in his SSC examinations, and then, God knows how, fell into bad company and became part of a gang of pickpockets; he began to pick people's pockets in trains and buses. He was caught one day and sent to a children's home. How long could Aslam wait for Jamila? One day, he married his uncle's daughter in Pune and began to work in some school there. One day, one of Jamila's sisters, Akhtari, who was studying in a college, went out and never came back. It turned out she had run off with a good-for-nothing boy from their neighbourhood. The other two sisters, too, failed in their respective classes and began to sit at home.

Three years have passed. The mother, stricken by paralysis, is lying in bed waiting for Death to claim her. But Death stands at the doorway, refusing to come in. At first, the mother would look at Jamila and cry, but by now her eyes have become desolate, like dried-up lakes. She simply gazes unblinkingly at Jamila with her vacant eyes as she passes by. The silver strands in Jamila's hair are increasing. A year ago, while combing her hair in the morning, when she spotted the first silver strand, she received a jolt to her heart. That night, she cried a lot. The next day, she plucked out the silver strand with a lot of care and attention. But by now, there are many silver strands in her hair. She has stopped pulling them out. Earlier, when thoughts of Aslam troubled her, she would bury her face in a pillow and sob quietly. But with time, Aslam's face and features started to blur in her remembering. By now, every trace of the past has been erased from her heart.

Do you know Jamila? She lives a few houses away from you. You would certainly have seen her. But perhaps you don't recognize her, because she still wears the burqa and her face is covered by the niqab.

# WHAT HAPPENED ON THE SHIP

*Anwar Qamar*

THE MV *GANDHI* had set sail from the famous port of Kandla in Gujarat at 7.00 a.m. on its way towards the historic city of Kolkata in the state of West Bengal. The Arabian Sea was a bit rough; the wind too was strong. A seabird or two could be spotted circling the ship. It was 11.00 a.m. now. A hushed but angry conversation was taking place between the captain, Arsh-ur Rahman, and Chief Officer Bimal Dutt.

'Sir,' Bimal Dutt was saying, 'have you not seen *Schindler's List*?'

Turning the ship's wheel with a sharp twist to the left, the captain said, 'The two of us had seen it together, possibly at the

Metro theatre in Kolkata. But what has that got to do with any of this?'

'It is connected, and directly so, sir. Did Schindler's deputy, who was a Jew, not save the lives of his Jewish brethren?'

'He did, indeed, but Schindler had to pay a heavy price for saving those lives,' the captain spoke, keeping his hand steady on the wheel to maintain a straight course. And after a moment's pause, he said, 'Had he not paid a heavy price to the Nazis, in the form of cash and kind, many of those Jews would have perished in concentration camps.'

'Yes, sir, that is what I am saying too. And I am not saying it as a Muslim or a Hindu, but as a human being: take them to Kolkata. We will go there and see what the Marxist government does with them. I am certain they will be given asylum.'

A short while ago, the quartermaster had arrived with the information that the sound of a child crying could be heard from one of the containers in the cargo. When the captain had asked him to explain, he said, 'Someone has muffled the child. At first, I was scared at the sound of a child crying. What was a child doing there? And if it was crying, why was it muffled? Was somebody else in the container besides the child? So, I tiptoed away and came here to the bridge to report the matter to you.'

MV *Gandhi* was a somewhat battered old ship. It had been in need of repair for years. Captain Arsh-ur Rahman had received orders to take the ship for dry-docking at the Visakhapatnam port so that the old ship could be repaired from scratch; but those orders had since been rescinded at the last moment. The reason was that the ship's owners had bagged a contract from a Gujarat-based leather manufacturing company to carry a large cargo.

Narottam Das Purushottam Das was about a hundred-year-old shipping company whose owners had been working steadfastly on the business principles and values laid down by their forefathers. They had never tried to bypass or override the rules and regulations prescribed by the state government, nor had they ever attempted to take undue liberties with policies formulated by the central government.

Therefore, Captain Arsh-ur Rahman informed his company headquarters via the following fax message, seeking instructions as to what he should do: 'Approximately forty Gujarati refugees have stowed away in a cargo container. They include nine children, twenty-five women and eleven elderly men. There is no mention of this human cargo in the ship's logbooks. Kindly inform me as to exactly what I should do with them under the circumstances.'

A short while ago, the seal had been broken on Container Number 27. Then the lock had been opened and the bolt released. And as soon as Shamsi had opened the door, a sharp stench had assailed their senses. They had seen men, women and children, sitting in separate rows, trembling with fright. Their eyes were covered with their hands. God knows how long they had been confined in this pitch-black darkness and filth. The captain instructed his staff to take these people to an upper deck, bathe them and give them a light meal.

The office manager, Mr D'Costa, placed the fax received from MV *Gandhi* on the table of Chhabil Das, the director of the shipping company, and stood waiting to receive instructions. The director instantly called a meeting of the company's board of directors. The contents of the fax were read out forthwith to the assembled board. The director declared that, under the present circumstances, the captain was the one person best suited to take the right decision.

A certain Mr Oberoi spoke up: 'I am reminded of the incidents from fifty-five to sixty years ago, from the time of the partition of the country – how people had crossed borders on pony carts, horse carriages, on foot, in goods trains. These poor, unfortunate beings seem to be like them, or rather like us. Brother Chhabil Dasji, how can I narrate my journey from Toba Tek Singh to Amritsar and from Amritsar to Delhi? How much these eyes have seen! Even now, the very memory of it makes me sit up with dread in the middle of the night, and I begin to shout and scream as though I have seen a ghost.'

Chhabil Das sought the advice of Mr D'Costa. The manager said, 'I have been looking at the rules and regulations of the *All-India Maritime Manual* so that I could get some instant guidance from the procedure laid down for such eventualities. According to the rules laid down in 1973, it is clearly stated that once a ship has sailed from a port, if the captain gets information that any such person or persons, whose names are not mentioned in the list of passengers or in the ship's logbook, are found on board the ship, then, upon reaching the ship's destination, such a person or persons must be handed over to the concerned authorities. Otherwise, if the captain feels that, without wasting any further time he can return to the port from which the ship had set sail and where the person or persons had boarded the vessel, he should do so and then hand over the person or persons to the concerned authorities of that port.'

Chhabil Dasji said, 'All right, then ... Since the ship will reach Kolkata after seven days, it will be better if they turn back and return to Kandla. There, they should hand over the container to the custody of the port authorities.'

Seventy-five-year-old Oberoi Sahab, who was one of the directors, said, 'Chhabil Dasji, this is the safest route for us to take. To hand over the refugees to the Gujarat government is the easiest option. You know very well what they will do with these people. I had once read a collection of stories by the late Urdu writer, Krishan Chander. It was entitled *Hum Vahashi Hain* (We are Barbarians). I had written to Krishanji after reading the book: "*You have risen above the two major groupings of our subcontinent to write about the sectarian violence of 1947. You have introduced the reader to the barbarian hiding within the human heart; meeting that barbarian leaves the reader completely dumbfounded.*"

'Krishanji had responded to my letter saying: "*Both the groups were guilty of committing communal violence. Both had committed acts of arson and loot and plunder. Both were equally responsible for the rape and brutalization of women. But after having gone through so much, we should resolve never to commit such deeds again.*"

'So, Chhabil Dasji, please instruct Arsh-ur Rahman to proceed forthwith for Kolkata with the container. Let us see what our home ministry decides to do with them. By the time they reach Kolkata, we shall try to contact Mr Ahluwalia, the home secretary, and seek his advice.'

By the time a fax was received at MV *Gandhi*, duly signed by Chhabil Dasji, the ship had already turned to go back towards Kandla. That is because Arsh-ur Rahman was a senior and much-experienced captain, well versed in the rules of the shipping trade.

He showed Bimal Dutt the fax and said, 'This world never gives anyone the opportunity to prove their neutrality. It isn't as though all the people in the container are my brothers and sisters. Why would I have shown them any preferential treatment? It is a good thing that this order has come.'

'Sir, we had discretionary powers. But you chose not to exercise your rights,' Bimal Dutt answered.

Arsh-ur Rahman smiled and said, 'All right, go and see if we have enough food and water.'

Suddenly, Shamsi came running to the bridge.

'What is the matter, Shamsi? Why do you look so agitated?'

Sir … Sir … From Container Number 16 too … I have just heard the sound of a child crying!'

# THE LINE

*Tariq Chhatari*

JUST BEFORE SETTING, the sun had hung peculiar banners in the clouded sky. These banners were red and also yellow. The sky seemed to be divided into twin-coloured bands. A dark line could be seen where the two colours met. If you looked closely, you could also see some white shadows lurking close by. With even the slightest quiver in the white shadows, the red and yellow colours seemed to darken, and a strange primeval fear seemed to percolate in the atmosphere. Never before had such strange white shadows appeared in the sky above this hamlet, nor had they ever managed to so neatly divide the sky into red and yellow bands. But today…

This fearsome evening had not had an ominous morning. Though the sky had been overcast from the start, the clouds were not dark. As the day wore on, a large white cloud, which was white on the surface but hid an inky blackness in its bosom, had drifted up from the west and spread itself gradually over the entire sky. Until then, small tufts of clouds had been frolicking among themselves, just like the Hindus and Muslims, who hopped and skipped across the line of communal differences, lived and played together in the hamlet. It was the seventh day in the month of Bhadon, and the temple was being decorated for tomorrow – for Krishna Ashtami, the birth of the Lord. In the small room below the temple, the idol was being dressed in all its finery and placed in the gaily coloured and brightly festooned little crib. The Lord would be born at the stroke of midnight – everyone, Hindus and Muslims alike, knew that.

'No, no, Hameed … not so high,' squealed Kusum, and Hameed immediately slowed the swing. Kusum was Pandit Brij Kishore's darling daughter. As she got off the rope swing dangling from a branch of the neem tree, Hameed took out a handful of ripe neem berries from the pocket of his kurta and gave them to her. She loved to eat those luscious berries, almost as much as Hameed loved to play the flute. Pandit Brij Kishore turned around as the first notes of Hameed's flute reached his ears. Kusum was filling a brass pitcher with water and Hameed was sitting at the edge of the well, playing the flute with his eyes closed. Panditji smiled, got up and walked to the well. Placing his hand on Hameed's head, he said, 'Truly, you are Kanhaiya … my Kanhaiya. This time, I will dress you as Kanhaiya and make you sit in the Janmashtami procession.'

And Hameed felt as though he was sitting, not beside the well, but in the golden chariot, playing his flute, and all around him were the fair maidens of Vrindavan. He searched the crowd for Kusum. He looked again and saw a group of women wearing silken ghararas and dupattas, reciting a milaad. Kusum was sitting beside his Amma Jaan. When several women started singing together, he could see Kusum's lips also moving. She seemed to be singing along with the other women. The flute still rested on his lips. Was he playing the flute or was it the sound of Kusum singing the milaad? He didn't know. Then there was a clamour – inside of him and outside. It was the sound of children's voices. Perhaps school had just got over and the children were scrambling home. Hameed suddenly came to his senses and began to walk behind Pandit Brij Kishore.

Hameed was the son of Faqir Muhammad. He had run away from his school at the mosque to sit in his neighbour Pandit Brij Kishore's pathshala. Pandit Brij Kishore loved him dearly, more than all his other pupils, and affectionately called him Kanhaiya. Hameed dreamt of Krishna and the Ashtami festival, and rocked his thoughts like the idol of infant Krishna being rocked in its gilded crib.

Panditji was standing in the sanctum in front of Krishan Bhagwan's image. Hameed paused at the doorway and looked closely at the Lord with the flute at His lips. Panditji offered water to the deity, lit the lamp, and closed his eyes in prayer. Hameed said his own prayer: 'Please, Allah Miyan, let the Ashtami come quickly, let me wear the tiara and become Kanhaiya and play the flute…' He crossed his left foot with his right and stood on tiptoe. He felt like taking the flute from the idol inside the temple and resting it against his own pursed lips. But his heart was aflutter. He could hear the sound of distant thunder. He looked up and saw banks of dark clouds rumbling and growling in the sky. Soon, it would rain. It was only appropriate that it should, for wasn't Kanhaiya born on just such a dark, rainy night? Soon the women of the hamlet would go for a ritual washing of His soiled diapers.

At last, night came. How eagerly he had been waiting for it! Tomorrow was Janmashtami. His uneasiness left him, and he felt light and joyful. The sleep from Hameed's eyes changed magically into the lilting notes of Krishna's flute. The flute played on and on, all night long, and Hameed hopped and skipped in the temple courtyard like the playful waves of the Jamuna River. The premises housed the temple itself, a courtyard, and a high-roofed veranda. In a corner stood a gleaming palanquin mounted on a brass-plated chariot, an elaborate four-legged affair burnished with ornate, beautifully embossed brass plates. Hameed danced over and stood close by the palanquin. Then he sat down, and felt the aeons passing by. He felt as though he was growing taller and bigger and mightier. On his finger was a chakra that whirled with amazing speed. Hameed could feel his own being dissolve and merge with every atom, every particle of the universe. His eyes were wide open. He could see everything in the world: the bright rays of the sun and the dense blackness of the night. Slowly, the night seeped into his eyes. As the cattle made their way to the fields with bells tinkling around their necks, and the muezzin in the mosque and the bells in the temple began to herald a new day, Hameed ran to seek shelter and sleep in Pandit Brij Kishore's lap.

In the morning, several well-meaning people from the hamlet assembled in the temple courtyard. Bakshiji, a pillar of the local community, asked Panditji, 'So, whom have you chosen to be the Child this time?'

Hameed's innocent pranks and guileless face danced before Pandit Brij Kishore's eyes. He said, 'Kanhaiya will be Krishna.' People looked at each other. Vaidji stuttered, 'Who? Kanhaiya?'

Panditji shook himself and said, 'I mean Hameed.'

'Hameed?!' Several people objected simultaneously. Then there was silence. Someone broke the silence. 'But the Child must be a Hindu!'

Before Pandit Brij Kishore could answer, Bakshiji pounced, 'But this is unheard of … How can you have a Muslim child as Krishanji on Ashtami?'

Seth Dungar Mal cleared his throat and said, 'It is all very well, Panditji, that we must abolish these differences of caste and creed, but…'

After a great deal of debate, the matter was settled. Hameed was chosen. But some people left the temple courtyard to show their displeasure.

The preparations began at noon. Panditji bathed Hameed, and then began the elaborate ritual of dressing him. First, a light dye made of indigo was patted all over his body. A lead oxide that gave off a faint, effulgent shade of pink was soaked, then ground to a paste and rubbed on Hameed's face. As the paste began to dry, a pale blue and pink powder was dusted over it. A glittering belt encircled his waist, a necklace gleamed around his throat, and a brocade tiara glowed on his head. There was also a flute in his hand, and a multicoloured chunri was looped from his left shoulder to his waist.

Pandit Brij Kishore had transformed his Kanhaiya into the real Krishan Bhagwan. Hands folded, he bowed before his Lord.

And then the wheels of the chariot began to move. At the head of the procession walked six groups of singers, and beside the palanquin, Panditji himself, holding a tray of offerings. The devout came in hordes, with offerings and flowers, clamouring to touch the Lord's feet and receive His blessings. By the time the procession wound its way through the narrow paths and alleys and reached the mosque, the sun too had nearly finished its trek across the skies. The muezzin was waiting for the procession to pass before he called the faithful to the evening prayer. The procession stopped beside the mosque. The kirtan singers sang with gusto. Panditji blew the conch shell with all his might. At the sound of the conch, the drummers stepped up the tempo. From the heart of this cacophony, a horrendous cry rang out as a stone, pelted from the direction of the mosque, hit Krishan Bhagwan squarely on the head and drew a blood-red line across his forehead. The blood from Krishan Bhagwan's forehead spurted, snuffing out the lamp in the ceremonial tray. The stone had been aimed at Krishan Bhagwan. It wounded Hameed. And innocent Kanhaiya's blood snuffed out the lamp for the puja.

Chaos broke out. Loud, hysterical voices crying for blood besieged the homes of Muslims. People swarmed towards the mosque. Pandit Brij Kishore plunged through the crowds to find a young man hacking away at the door of the mosque with an axe. He snatched the axe away. The air was rent by the cry 'Nara-e-Takbir … Allah-o-Akbar!'[1] He ran towards the sound and saw Seth Dungar Mal and Ramanand trying to pacify the crowd.

1 Literally meaning 'The Shout of Allah is Great!', it is usually the rallying cry from a Muslim group during a communal riot.

'Brother, what is this? We are brothers, aren't we? We were born on this soil, and we shall…'

'And we shall die on this soil!' came the scream. Brutish rage and terror took over. Seth Dungar Mal and Ramanand were killed. Now, there was no stopping the mobs. No one knew what would happen next. Panditji ran towards the house of Banda Khan from where he could hear jubilant cries of 'Jai Bajrang Bali'.[2] He found Banda Khan's doorway spewing flames and heard the piteous cries of women and children trapped behind that wall of fire. Panditji looked at the mob. Fear and horror were in their eyes. They seemed to be asking: 'What's happening? This shouldn't be happening.' But still, it was happening. It was as though something was going on right in front of their eyes without their wanting it to. But how? And why? What was this force that was invisible yet caused all this…

In the midst of it all, Panditji noticed that several people were looking up at the sky. The sky that sheltered them was today adorned in the most peculiar colours. It was streaked with red and also yellow. A dark line could be seen where the two colours met. If you looked closely, you could see some white shadows lurking close by. The red and yellow colours seemed to darken with the slightest quiver in the white shadows, and a strange primeval fear seemed to percolate in the atmosphere. Never before had such strange white shadows appeared in the sky above this hamlet, nor had they ever managed to so neatly divide the sky into red and yellow bands. But today…

---

2 Literally meaning 'Victory to Hanuman!', it is usually the rallying cry from the Hindu side during a communal riot.

Pandit Brij Kishore ran towards the palanquin. A man had picked up the axe from beside Krishan Bhagwan – it was the ceremonial axe with which the Lord slew Evil – and he stood waving it before a terrified Kanhaiya. Every year, the sharp-edged axe was kept in the palanquin, and at the end of the Ashtami procession, Krishan Bhagwan slew the evil Kansa, thus symbolizing the victory of good over evil.

A muffled cry escaped Panditji's lips, 'What is this … this is Krishan Bhagwan … our Kanhaiya.'

Har Prasad had just sung the aarti. Now he spoke in a dull, flat voice, 'No … this is Hameed. Faqir Muhammad's son.'

Several people spoke up. 'Yes, yes, this is Hameed, the son of a Musalman. They have insulted our Krishan Bhagwan. They threw a stone at the palanquin. It hit Bhagwanji. Look at the blood dripping from his forehead. And now these cowards are hiding in their homes.'

The man with the axe swung it in the air and roared, 'We will avenge this outrage. Today we will…'

'No…' Panditji shouted and lunged at the axe. The man threw Panditji down from the palanquin and struck Hameed a mighty blow.

Resplendent, glowing, Krishan Bhagwan fell … scattering the shining tiara, the spangled necklace, and the glittering waistband. A thin, red line formed on the ground. Some people stood on one side of the line, some on the other. There was clamour on both sides. It was difficult to tell whether the noise was greater on this side or on the other.

# THE VULTURES OF DOONGERWADI

*Ali Imam Naqvi*

THE TWO OF them were flabbergasted by the strange happening. Without quite meaning to, they put the stretcher down on the ground. They looked at the corpse in amazement. Then their glances met, and their eyes asked many questions of each other. For a long time, the orbs of their eyes kept moving in their sockets, and when they paused, the two shrugged their shoulders to show their ignorance. In unison, they stretched the muscles in their neck and turned their jaws, first to the left and then to the right.

Then their eyes turned upwards to circle the dense trees at the edge of the doongerwadi.[1]

Not a single vulture could be seen until far into the distance. It was the first time such a thing had happened.

The warning bell had rung two hours ago. Fifteen minutes later, the helpers in Bungli Number 2 had given the corpse in their safekeeping. They had brought the corpse within the safe walls of the tower and shut the gates. Then, opening the small window in the door, Firoz Bhatena had looked out at the mourners and made enquiries about the deceased.

'What about some tip…?'

The attendant smiled and placed two ten-rupee notes for Bhatena. He immediately put one in his own shirt and, extending the other note towards Hormuz, shut the window.

'O Lord…' Hormuz raised his head and looked towards the sky peeping through the dense foliage on the tall and majestic trees. Then, he signalled Bhatena with his eyes; both bent and picked up the stretcher and began to move towards the tower.

'Firoz…' Bhatena addressed his companion as they walked.

'Hunn…'

'How long … how long are we going to do this work?'

---

1 Doongerwadi, literally meaning 'garden on the hill', was the name of a piece of land on which a tower of silence was built by the Parsi community in Malabar Hill, Mumbai; it has since become a generic word and come to be used almost synonymously with the tower of silence. The doongerwadi compound includes the bungli, an antechamber where the corpse is kept and the last rituals are observed. From the bungli, the corpse is taken to the actual tower, where vultures will pick it clean.

'Come on, come on, don't chew my brain.'

'Is this the only work we are fit to do?'

'What do you think?'

'I don't know … I am just asking.'

'Yes.'

'I swear by Zarathustra,' and he raised his eyes heavenwards as he swore. For a couple of minutes, both were quiet; then, Bhatena said, 'Look here, Hormuz, the Parsi Panchayat[2] raised us. What can we do if our destiny is flawed? Do you understand or not? Tell me.'

'That's your story, brother. But to tell you the truth, I am quite fed up … fed up of this life.'

But the chain of their conversation broke. They had reached the tower. With one nudge from Hormuz's foot, the door to the tower flung open and, in the next moment, they were inside – with one standing at the head of the corpse and the other at its feet. The dead person's face, smeared in curd, looked white. Hormuz raised the head a little, while Bhatena whipped the shroud off the body. Then they took turns to touch the corpse's feet and brought the hands to the eyes and chest. Then, both stood aside. By way of covering, the corpse had only a handkerchief tied around its waist. Hormuz and Bhatena left the handkerchief where it was, turned around and left the tower.

They returned to their room and sat on two chairs beside a table. Hormuz took out a bottle of alcohol and kept it on the table. Both took turns filling their glasses. Firoz Bhatena put a piece of patrail in his mouth and said, 'Hormuz!'

---

2 The apex body representing the Parsi Zoroastrian community in a city.

'Yes?'

'What a life!'

'What happened?'

'Tower ... One ... Two ... Four ... and...'

'Yes, and?'

'What else.'

'And corpse, corpse...'

'I don't understand.'

'Look at the life of a Parsi.'

'Life?'

'Yes.'

'Why? What happened?'

'Our youth is fast-paced but our old age is slow.'

'Yes, absolutely true.'

For a long time, the two sat talking idly, and drinking. After some time, they began to sob and cry. Suddenly, the bell rang; this time, the corpse was coming from Bungli Number 4.

'Good! The Lord Zarathustra has arranged for our drinks today!'

'Hurry up! Come on!'

They hurried towards the outer gate of the bungli. Once again, the door had been opened and an empty stretcher had been laid outside. In a short while, the corpse from Bungli Number 4 was given to their charge. Once again, the attendant had handed them two ten-rupee notes; this time, Hormuz had stepped forward and taken them. The door of the bungli was shut. The two of them picked up the stretcher and began to move outside.

'Hormuz!'

'Yes?'

'One day, we too shall go like this, won't we?'

Hormuz stopped in his tracks. He turned his head and looked at Firoz Bhatena. Then he asked in a terrified tone, 'Why did you ask this question?'

'Everyone has to die.'

'True, but I have no intention of dying just yet.'

'Intention? Well said, brother!'

'Shut up, you scum! What have we seen in our life so far? Corpses, corpses, and more corpses, and vultures and, at the most, cheap liquor from the roadside stall with a dash of pungent rock salt! Ten-rupee notes … I ask you: isn't there more to life than this?'

Firoz made no answer to this. He kept looking at Hormuz.

'Tell me, brother, is this all there is to life?'

'What can I say? All I know is that if we have come, we must go too one day. And when I go, someone else will come in my place.'

'Shut up, you sister-fucking bastard!' Hormuz screamed.

'Don't shout, brother. And don't talk about life; we are carrying a corpse in our hands.'

They walked till the tower in silence, and when the gate of the tower opened…

The two of them were flabbergasted by the strange happening. Without quite meaning to, they put the stretcher down on the ground. They looked at the corpse in amazement. Then their glances met, and their eyes asked many questions of each other. For a long time, the orbs of their eyes kept moving in their sockets, and when they paused, the two shrugged their shoulders to show their ignorance … Then their eyes turned upwards to circle the dense trees at the edge of the doongerwadi.

And it was the first time such a thing had happened that the vultures were missing and the corpse was lying there intact. For what had been happening all this while was that the corpse would be laid out, Firoz and Hormuz would leave the tower, and in about twenty or twenty-five minutes, the corpse would be transferred into the bellies of the vultures. They would see the vultures flying away, then go into the tower, soak the skeletal remains with acid, whereupon they would turn into ash and run down the channels into the deep pits under the tower – deep down, God knows how far, into the innards of the earth. Sometimes, it so happened that no corpse would come. At such times, the panchayat would buy a goat for the vultures and give it to Hormuz and Bhatena, to stop the vultures from flying away for want of sustenance. But today was the strangest sight ever! The corpse was lying there intact, and the vultures were missing!

Hormuz and Bhatena kept looking at each other with their eyes wide open. After standing still with amazement for some time, they deposited the second corpse, too, on the grille of the tower. Then they looked at each other with many questions in their eyes.

'What do you think? Should we tell Kaikubad?'

'Yes, we should.'

They reached their room and pressed the emergency switch. A red bulb fitted on the wall of the doongerwadi began to flicker. Surprised, the clerks came out of their office. And the bulbs for each of the bunglis, too, began to flicker. The priests stopped their chanting. The dogs roaming around here and there in the bunglis stopped and cowered. The mourners who had come with the new corpses were bewildered; they, too, came out of the bunglis. Everywhere, there was the same question on everyone's lips: 'What happened? What happened?'

Kaikubad ran out and looked at the sky; then he turned back. Everyone surrounded him. 'What happened? What happened?' These words echoed all around. In response, Kaikubad announced, 'The vultures have gone.'

'The vultures have gone?'

'The vultures have gone?'

'But why?'

'Something must have happened!'

'But what could have happened?'

The secretary of the Parsi Panchayat received Kaikubad's phone call and his forehead creased with a network of frowns. He heard the entire story, put the receiver back in its cradle, and informed the director through the intercom. Immediately, an urgent meeting was called. The matter was placed before the board of directors. But the question still remained: 'Where had the vultures gone?'

'What did you say? The vultures have gone?' There was the slightest trace of disbelief in the police commissioner's voice.

'Yes, our vultures have gone,' the president of the Parsi Panchayat stressed each syllable and repeated his statement. Then he listened to what the police commissioner had to say with rapt attention. The colour came and went from his face. He kept listening to the police commissioner for a very long time. When the story ended on the other side, he put the receiver back in its cradle. All the other directors were looking at him. He gave them the gist of his conversation with the police commissioner. Though everyone came out of the meeting with some amount of satisfaction, they carried within them a far greater number of worries. The secretary called the doongerwadi. Kaikubad conveyed the gist of the conversation between the president of the Parsi Panchayat and the police commissioner to the honourable priests and the assembled mourners. The news reached Hormuz and Bhatena from the priests, via the attendants of the bungli. Bhatena heard the entire matter with the closest attention. Then he began to look up at the sky. From the windows and through the dense foliage on the trees, the sky could be seen clearly. There were no crows or kites, nor vultures.

And then they were startled. The warning bell was ringing. A corpse was coming from Bungli Number 3. Once again, they found themselves standing at the door of the bungli. The corpse arrived. This time, the attendant extended two fifty-rupee notes towards Bhatena. Taking the corpse inside the tower, Bhatena made a face and said, 'Hormuz!'

'Speak, brother.'

'Why are all the Parsis dying today?'

Hormuz made no answer to this question. He was looking up at the sky. 'There is not a bird in sight, and the corpses are piling up one after the other.'

'But where have the birds gone?'

'The police commissioner said that all the vultures have gone to the Sunday and Monday markets.'

'But why?'

'Arre, those Hindus and Muslims have fought with each other. There have been riots. They have burnt the hearse van, and also the ambulance. The road is littered with corpses, and our vultures are having a feast. And that police commissioner, he said that once the roads have been cleared, our vultures are going to return on their own.'

'So what if the roads clear ... Will the vultures return? ... After all, this is India ... There is a riot here every day. Everyday there is burning and arson, everyday people die ... What then? ... What the hell! ... Will the vultures ever return?'

# ACKNOWLEDGEMENTS

I AM DEEPLY GRATEFUL to each of the authors included in this anthology for trusting me with their work. In some instances where the author is no longer with us, I am indebted to their literary heirs for granting me permission to translate the writings of their near and dear ones.

Of the translations included here, my translations of Tariq Chhatari's 'The Line' and Ali Imam Naqvi's 'The Vultures of Doongerwadi' first appeared in *Pigeons of the Domes: Stories on Communalism*, edited and introduced by me and published by Niyogi Books in 2015. The copyright for these translations rests with me, and fresh permission has been taken from Tariq Chhatari and the son and heir of Ali Imam Naqvi to include both stories in this volume. Also, my translation of 'A Night's Paradise' by Faiyaz Riffat first appeared in *New Urdu Writings: Stories from India and Pakistan*, edited by me and published by Tranquebar in 2013. The volume is since out of print and its rights have been returned to me. Fresh permission was taken from the son and heir of Faiyaz Riffat for including this translation in the present volume.

# ABOUT THE WRITERS

**Surendra Prakash**, born in Faislabad, Pakistan, won the Sahitya Akademi Award in 1989 for his collection of short stories entitled *Baazgoi*. His other outstanding collections include: *Doosre Aadmi ka Drawing Room*, *Barf par Mukaalma* and *Haazir Haal Jaari*. Interestingly, he did not have a formal education. He is known for the highly perceptive symbolism in his stories. He died in 2002 in Mumbai.

**Qurratulain Hyder** was a Jnanpith Award winning Urdu prose writer, best known for her novels *Aag ka Darya, Mere Bhi Sanamkhane, Akhir-e Shab ke Humsafar* and the collection of short stories entitled *Patjhar ki Awaaz*. Daughter of pioneer fiction-writer parents, she herself is considered a prose stylist of great acclaim and originality.

**Ghazanfar** is ex-director of the Academy of Professional Development of Urdu Medium Teachers, Jamia Millia Islamia, New Delhi. His work includes the novels *Pani*, *Divya Bani* and *Manjhi*, and the short-story collections *Hairat Farosh* and *Parking Area*. He was awarded the Iqbal Samman (2018) by the government of Madhya Pradesh, the Bihar Urdu Academy Award (2016) and the Uttar Pradesh Urdu Academy Award (2020). He served as member of the Jnanpith committee from 2011 to 2014, and as jury member of the Iqbal Samman.

**Zakia Mashhadi** hails from an urban, educated, middle-class family with roots in western Uttar Pradesh. She did her BA and MA in psychology from Lucknow University in 1966. An avid reader, she started her writing career in 1974 and has since published five collections of short stories in Urdu and translated more than a dozen books for prestigious literary organizations like the Sahitya Akademi, the National Book Trust, and the Khuda Bakhsh Oriental Public Library, Patna, from English and Hindi into Urdu, and vice versa. She has also written more than a dozen booklets for rural neo-literates in simple Hindi and Urdu.

Poet, author, film-maker and lyricist, **Gulzar** is one of the most prominent names in cinema, popular culture and literature in present-day India. Recipient of the Padma Bhushan and the Sahitya Akademi Award, he has also received an Oscar for the song '*Jai ho!*' in the Hollywood film *Slumdog Millionaire* in 2008, and the Dadasaheb Phalke Award for his contribution to the Indian film industry in 2014. A well-respected name in poetry circles, he has several non-film short-story and poetry collections to his credit. He has recently published his translations of Rabindranath Tagore and has written poetry especially for children.

Born in 1952 in Andhwas (Nalanda), **Abdus Samad** served as a professor of political science and principal of two different colleges. He has written twelve novels and seven collections of short stories in Urdu. His awards include the Sahitya Akademi Award (1990), the Bhartiya Bhasha Parishad Award (1998), a lifetime achievement award from the Bihar Urdu Academy (2016), the Ghalib Award (2014), the Farogh-e-Urdu Adab Award (2017), among others.

**Syed Muhammad Ashraf** was born in Sitapur, a town in the Awadh region of Uttar Pradesh, and belongs to a family of devout scholars and Sufi saints of Marehra Shareef, district Etah, UP. Having retired as chief commissioner of income tax in Kolkata, he has steadfastly balanced his career as a senior officer in the Indian Revenue Service along with his literary and academic interests. His major work includes two collections of short stories, *Daar se Bichchre* (1994) and *Baad-e Saba ka Intizar* (2000) for which he received the Sahitya Akademi Award, and the novels *Numbardar ka Neela* (1997) and *Aakhri Sawariyan* (2016).

Born in Etawah, Uttar Pradesh, **Faiyaz Riffat** did an MA in political science and worked in radio and television. He was director of Lucknow Doordarshan. His works include two short-story collections, *Naye Ahd-Naame ki Saughaat* (1975) and *Mere Hisse ka Zehr* (1997), and a collection of poetry, *Beetee Ruton ka*

*Manzar* (1996), for which he was awarded by the Urdu Academies of Maharashtra and UP. His latest novel is *Banaraswali Gali*.

Born in 1963 in Bareilly, Uttar Pradesh, **Khalid Jawed** is an award-winning fiction writer in Urdu. His collection of short stories titled *Akhri Dawat* was published from Penguin India Ltd. He received the Katha Award in 1997 for his story '*Bure Mausam Mein*'. His writings have been translated into English, Hindi, French and Spanish. He works as professor in the department of Urdu, Jamia Millia Islamia, New Delhi. His novel *Nematkhana*, published as *The Paradise of Food* in English, won the fifth JCB Prize for Literature.

Shaikh Abdussalam Abdurrazzaq, born in Panvel, Maharashtra, and better known by his pen name **Salam Bin Razzaq**, is a Mumbai-based Urdu and Hindi short-story writer and translator. His short-story collection *Shikasta Buton ke Darmiyan* won the 2004 Sahitya Akademi Award for Urdu.

**Anwar Qamar** has written over two hundred short stories which have appeared in the following collections: *Chandni ke Supurd* (1978), *Chaupal mein Suna Hua Qissa* (1984), *Colour Blind* (1990), *Jahaz par Kya Hua* (2008). He lives in Mumbai.

**Khurshid Akram** belongs to the generation of Urdu writers who came to the fore during the 1990s. He has two volumes each of short stories (*Ek Ghair Mashroot Muafinama* and *Raat ki Baat*), poetry (*Pichhli Peet ke Kaaraney* and *Nazm Kuchh aur Chahti Hai*), and criticism (*Andaz-e-Nazar Mera* and *Musafirat ke Marhale*). A number of his stories, translated into English, Hindi, Odia, Punjabi and other Indian languages, have appeared in various anthologies.

He has also translated books into Urdu from Hindi, Bangla and English. Akram was the editor of the prestigious Urdu literary magazine *Aajkal*. Born in Calcutta in 1963, he has been living in Delhi since 1987.

**Tariq Chhatari** retired as professor and chairperson from the department of Urdu, Aligarh Muslim University. Born in Chhatari, Bulandshahr district, Uttar Pradesh, he began his career as a programme executive in All India Radio in 1984. His notable contributions include a collection of short stories entitled *Bagh ka Darwaza* (2001) and *Jadeed Afsana: Hindi–Urdu*, a comparative study of Hindi–Urdu short stories after 1960, for which he received the Uttar Pradesh Urdu Akademi Award. He is also the recipient of the lifetime achievement award for fiction given by the Uttar Pradesh Urdu Akademi. His recent publications include a collection of his articles titled *Bagh ka Dusra Darwaza*, compiled by Dr Ahsan Ayyubi.

**Ali Imam Naqvi** was a noted fiction writer of modern times who began his writing career around 1970. '*Khiltey Huwey Bil*' was his first story that brought him to the notice of readers. In 1980, he published his first story collection entitled *Naye Makaan ki Deemak*, going on to publish four more collections: *Mubahilah, Ghatte Badhtey Saaye, Mausam Azaabon Ka*, and *Kahi Ankahi*. Naqvi also wrote the novels *Teen Batti ke Rama* and *Bisaat*.

# ABOUT THE EDITOR AND TRANSLATOR

**Dr Rakhshanda Jalil** is an award-winning translator, writer and literary historian. She has published over thirty books and written over fifty academic papers and essays. Her book on the lesser-known monuments of Delhi, *Invisible City*, continues to be a bestseller. Her other books include: *Liking Progress, Loving Change: A Literary History of the Progressive Writers Movement in Urdu*; a biography of the Urdu feminist writer Dr Rashid Jahan, *A Rebel and Her Cause*; translations of *The Sea Lies Ahead*, Intizar Husain's seminal novel on Karachi, and Krishan Chander's Partition novel, *Traitor*; an edited volume of critical writings on Ismat Chughtai titled *An Uncivil Woman*; a literary biography of the Urdu poet Shahryar; *The Great War: Indian Writings on the First World War*; *Preeto & Other Stories: The Male Gaze in Urdu*; *Kaifiyat*, a translation of Kaifi Azmi's poems; *Jallianwala Bagh: Literary Responses in Prose & Poetry*; *Footprints on Zero Line: Writings on the Partition*, a translation of short stories and poems by Gulzar; a collection of essays on identity, culture, politics and literature entitled *But You Don't Look Like a Muslim*. She runs an organization called Hindustani Awaaz, devoted to the popularization of Hindi–Urdu literature and culture.

# HarperCollins *Publishers* India

At HarperCollins India, we believe in telling the best stories and finding the widest readership for our books in every format possible. We started publishing in 1992; a great deal has changed since then, but what has remained constant is the passion with which our authors write their books, the love with which readers receive them, and the sheer joy and excitement that we as publishers feel in being a part of the publishing process.

Over the years, we've had the pleasure of publishing some of the finest writing from the subcontinent and around the world, including several award-winning titles and some of the biggest bestsellers in India's publishing history. But nothing has meant more to us than the fact that millions of people have read the books we published, and that somewhere, a book of ours might have made a difference.

As we look to the future, we go back to that one word—a word which has been a driving force for us all these years.

Read.

Harper Collins · 4th · HARPER PERENNIAL · HARPER BUSINESS · HARPER BLACK · हार्पर हिन्दी

HarperCollins *Children's Books* · HARPER DESIGN · HARPER VANTAGE · Harper Sport